The
Rescued
Heart

The Rescued Heart

by ANNABEL *and* EDGAR JOHNSON

Harper & Brothers   *Publishers*   New York

To

Mary and John Rossier

PART
I

Christie

1

The black Thunderbird scatted in and out, flipping its tail at the bigger cars that cluttered up the Hollywood Freeway on a Sunday afternoon. With the top peeled back, a slipstream of warm air raked the two young people in the front seat. The boy driving was dark and taut; the girl who sat beside him seemed like the brightest part of the day.

Borne along on the channel of traffic that poured in-bound through Cahuenga Pass, she was like a small chip of gold, the pale blond hair tumbling about her face and such a radiance in her look, it might almost have been a gift of the sunlight—if there'd been such brilliance that afternoon. But the sun was an orange ball painted on a sky thick with smog; the foothills above the Pass were faint outlines sketched behind the brown-stained air. And so the tired Sunday drivers looked at the girl instead, and smiled as the little car raced past. A few shook their heads when it swerved and darted recklessly from one lane to another, scattering music behind it. When a slow ballad came on the air, the boy reached forward and twisted the dial impatiently.

"That's from nowhere."

As he searched for a new station, he was steering one-handed through a narrow spot in the crush. The girl caught her breath and held it until they were clear again.

Not that she was afraid. Christie wasn't sure just what it was she felt. The excitement of going some place fast, any place, to be on the move, leaving the drudges behind —that was part of it. But the risk was the real challenge, the near-miss, the streaking along one roaring inch away from the rest of the mad race. It was like taking a dare—it gave her a charge through all the wires that kept her strung tight inside. A burning that drove off the chilly dread of being slow and dull. These days she didn't feel alive until the needle hit sixty.

As they came into the interchange, the boy eased up suddenly, dawdling along at forty-five.

Restlessly Christie said, "Hey, Rue', are we out of gear?"

He shook his head. "I got a cop looking over my shoulder." Glancing up irritably at the police helicopter that hovered above, he told it softly, "Go on, flap off,

4

lousy law." But he kept to one lane.

For all that he was the cautious type, Rudy had more temper than some. So many boys were sloppy, with a head start on middle-aged spread. If he wasn't handsome, at least Rudy was neat—always kept his flat-top in trim —and there was a moodiness about his look, a kind of discontent that had struck an answering note in Christie ever since that first date. And yet his rebellion never quite clenched up.

Maybe, she thought, it was because there never really was anything solid to fight. Life seemed to muddle along in a rut; the daily scramble was so complicated that you couldn't attack it. School never was so bad that you had to do something about it—teachers were all right. Even parents were fairly nice, or trying to be. Most of the time.

So when the desperate feeling came over her, of being somehow trapped, needing to beat her way out of a corner, Christie had to admit it was too shadowy to lay hold of. Except now; now they'd have something concrete to grapple with. Today, all at once, the whole situation had got out of its rut and come rushing at her. As soon as they got to the beach, she would tell Rudy; he'd come to her rescue, together they'd plan some way out. . . .

"The law has left, Rue'," she said impatiently. "Let's pick up an axle."

They were coming out onto the long straightaway of the Harbor Freeway. Rudy eased his foot down and the

5

T-Bird took off, its dual exhausts making a blast, a going-away sound that was part of the thrill of thrust.

Christie faced into the wind blindly, wishing they could just once go fast enough!

Of course, Christie realized that she had to be careful in telling Rudy the news. It could come out sounding dismal, and of all sins that was the worst.

As she sat there that afternoon, looking out across the beach with its layer of people laid out like a million strips of half-cooked bacon curling up on a huge griddle, she was thinking of the competition. The world was so full of girls with the kind of dimensions that boys drool over that Christie had to be twice as careful not to sound any sour notes.

Years ago, when she had reached the age of self-recognition, Christie had looked in the mirror and known she wasn't going to make out on looks. Her face was too well defined for a girl: humorous, angular, the mouth too broad to be classic, eyes not blue enough—just a sort of changeable hazel. She had always been too slender. Some people called her "fragile," but the less kind ones said she was just plain skinny. So all in all, it had been one long uphill road to make the rest of the kids forget that she wasn't a real doll. It meant she had to spark the parties, think up new tricks, make with the quick joke—pass the laughs. Kit, the kidder—that was her role, the reason Rudy had asked her to go steady.

The real test had come when she'd had that awful,

stupid fainting spell in class a few weeks ago. A thing like that would have dimmed most girls' reputations; it was enough to give people a creepy feeling about you. But the kids had thought it was some kind of gag at first, something to irritate the teacher. By the time they found out it was for real, she had been right side up again. Of course, the folks had almost queered things all over by sending her to the hospital for a checkup, but she had even managed to turn that into something of a riot. Everybody had sent her "get sick" cards, she'd written silly wish-you-were-here notes, made out a Last Will, and really hammed it up. Christie felt rather proud to think how they had all forgiven the episode. A wonderful bunch of kids!

But she was also ready to admit that if she ever turned off the shimmer, they would flock away from her just as fast. Even Rudy. She looked down at him anxiously; he lay stretched out on his back, but hardly at ease. His hands kept twitching and every few minutes he spun the dial of the portable. Christie understood. The right kind of beat going in the background steadies you, helps you find a rhythm inside. Without it, you get fidgety. Only right now she wished she could think a minute.

"... Only sixteen, she was only sixteen ..." somebody sang. The lyrics prickled her like hot sand.

"Rue'," she said cautiously, "dim the tune a minute. I need some advice—father-and-mother type."

He turned the volume down. "You got parent trouble? You?"

She nodded. "They just hit me with ten tons of news this morning. Seems we're leaving town, moving out of Los Angeles. Everything down the skids—school, friends, good times. Dad's given notice that we'll be out of the apartment by the end of October."

"Holy cat! That's less than two weeks!" Rudy hitched up on his elbows, aghast. Then, suddenly, his look turned suspicious. "You pulling another one of your gags?"

"I'm pulling my hair, dear," she told him firmly. "This is for real."

"They can't *do* that."

She shrugged. "They're going to. It's Dad's health. Seems that when I was in the hospital that time, he was having some checkups, too. The doctors say the smog is poisoning him or something, he has to get away from it. So we're all going out into the desert and—just—dry up, or whatever you do in the desert."

"I don't get it. You mean like to a dude ranch?"

"Nothing like that." Christie didn't dare tell him about the house trailer. She could imagine what he'd think of that! She flipped like a coin inside every time she thought of it herself. "The idea is for us to settle down in some little town. Dad says he wants peace and quiet."

"And send you to some hick school in the sticks!"

"Dad says if this is just some crossroads with no school at all, he doesn't think it will hurt me to miss a year."

"Oh, no. No. No, he can't do that." Rudy squirmed over onto his stomach, his back all furry with sand. It was fiercely hot for October—really cruel. All at once

8

Christie wanted to push the heavy air away from her; it was like a suffocating blanket—she couldn't breathe—couldn't think—

"There's a law," he was going on, shaking a finger at her. "You got to let a kid go to school or they can put you in jail."

For some reason it struck her as funny, because of all people Rudy hated laws. So now he was digging up the legal angle, when anybody knows that parents have ways of getting around the laws that are made against kids. She started to laugh. . . .

"Did you tell him," Rudy said a little more urgently, "how it'll warp your personality? Your old man can read any of these head-shrinkers that write the columns in the papers. Besides, they say a high-school diploma means you'll earn $50,000 more in your lifetime. He can't turn down $50,000, can he? What's so funny?"

Because by now Christie was helpless in the clutch of her laughter and there really wasn't anything funny. She bent over, hugging her knees, the tears starting down her face. *What's the matter with me?* she wondered. *I can't stop!*

Rudy was shaking her lightly by the shoulder. "This is a gag. You been pulling my leg."

"I was never more serious in my life," she gasped hysterically. "But don't you see, Rue'? I've been sounding off practically every hour on the hour about what a drag school is and how I can't see it doing anybody any good. So now you think I'll fool anybody if I start

9

loving the dear old grind?" She wiped her eyes a little shakily. "Besides, Dad knows I hate this plan. It doesn't make any difference. They just don't care."

In spite of herself, Christie felt a momentary hatred for them. She supposed she ought to be worried about Dad, but he looked as healthy as a horse. And just about as unsympathetic. He hadn't even turned an eyelash at her frantic protests.

"Rue', what am I going to do?" Christie hadn't meant to say it like that, in a sort of semi-quaver.

"Well, you can leave, that's all. You're old enough. You can get a nice little place of your own, live your own life."

Christie hesitated. As a matter of fact, it was the first thing she'd thought of—an apartment where she could come and go as she pleased, decorate it herself. But the practical side kept fogging things up.

"What do I use for money?"

Rudy turned away and stared out at the sullen gray slick of the ocean shifting around out there in the dead light. There was annoyance in the pulled-down look of his mouth. Christie felt a little frightened—she shouldn't have mentioned money. Money was the dead end of this world. There never was enough. A tank of gas kills a five-dollar bill. A round of burgers and fries doesn't leave enough change to tip the carhop. One new dress and the allowance is absolutely shredded. So if you cut on out away from home and have no allowance, then what?

10

"People get jobs," Rudy said glumly.

"But I'd have to quit school to do that, too. And then I really would have the law down on me. The folks would—"

"Don't make it so complicated," he cut in sharply. "You just vanish. Take another name. So what if you skip school, who cares?"

She was a little shocked. She'd thought he would be the one to care most if she wasn't around to have lunch with, meet after class.

"Besides," she said, frowning, "I don't have any training for a job."

"Any yoyo can type." He spoke so shortly that Christie fell silent. The heat was really choking her. She couldn't seem to keep this sounding gay, and he was making it pretty clear that the subject was congealing him. She couldn't really blame him. Who wants to think about all this? It's too hopeless. The whole future is one long bind, grinding over installments that come due, hating some crummy job or, if you're in business for yourself like Dad, worrying all the time about rush orders, workmen quitting, taxes. By the time the government finishes picking up the stupid taxes, you'd be better off to go on relief. Or, as Rudy often said, just stay in the Army—they're going to chop off a couple of years for you anyway.

If she were a boy, Christie thought, she'd just as soon join the Army right this minute. But a girl has it so much worse. So many places you can't go alone, things you can't do. At least a boy can always get around, but a girl has to sit back and hope. It could be a long wait, too—it could be forever. If a girl doesn't attract people to her, she might as well give up and buy knitting needles.

Frantically Christie searched for something carefree and funny to say, to take the curse off the party, but it wouldn't come.

Finally Rudy turned to look at her, his eyes unsteady and disturbed. Leaning over, he reached up to pinch her ear fondly. "Listen, Kitten, this'll all work itself out. You can do anything—you're way out ahead. You've got what other girls are still looking for. Only just—you know—assert yourself or something. Don't let 'em take you away from me. You're a high note, way up high. You're the only thing that ever gets me off the ground."

With a surge of gratitude, Christie smiled, although her throat was all knotted up for some crazy reason. "Sure," she said in a wispy voice. "I guess we'll figure things out as we get to them."

"Figure?" He tugged at the little hair on the nape of her neck. "Figure nothing. It'll work out, I tell you. Everything works out if you give it time."

2

The heat hung on all that week, locked in the giant basin where the city sprawled, helpless, under the weight of it. The trapped fumes thickened until the acrid air brought tears to the eyes. On the palm trees the fronds hung motionless. And yet the city itself seemed to pulse more feverishly than ever.

Standing on a downtown corner, hemmed in by tall buildings and crisscrossing traffic, Christie felt almost afraid of this monster of a town. And yet, she thought, this is the way to come of age. How better can you break through into the grown-up part of the world than to step out and come to grips with Los Angeles? She even felt a certain desperate admiration for the complexity of it, sprawled out for miles in every direction, crammed with people—little people, big people, some of the biggest. How did they get on top? Lucky breaks? That was usually the starting place. But most of them had known rough times first, even hungry times.

Christie wondered what it would feel like—not to have enough money in her purse to buy dinner. She'd been trying to cope with a hundred uncertainties this week, and after her weary trek around town today she had to admit she was no nearer the answers.

The only thing she knew for sure was that she hated all adults. Everywhere. Why couldn't they be just human? And why did they all seem to detest young people so instantly? That wise look you get tossed at you: Go away, kid, don't bother me. Or the prissed-up sneer: These teenagers! Taking up our time with their silly questions! Why aren't they at home where they belong? Oh, it came across, all right.

You'd think it was a crime to want to get a job. The pained look on the face of the man in the employment agency when he'd asked for her social-security card—he obviously suspected that she didn't have one. He didn't believe the quick cover-up, either, when she'd told him she had just left it at home. He'd asked for local re-ferences, and when she fumbled he had turned away disgusted.

Not that she was defeated. There must be places where you didn't get all the cross-examination. In fact, that ad for the waitress had said specifically, "No previous experience necessary." The only reason, maybe,

14

that she didn't have a job right this minute was that when she'd got to the address, Christie had found it wasn't a restaurant, but a bar full of boozy-looking characters and she hadn't been able to summon the nerve to go in. Chicken, she accused herself scornfully.

One trouble was that she'd never before really thought about a job; she'd sort of pictured herself just getting married, having a family. Not necessarily with Rudy—in fact, she was beginning not to count on him for anything. It would have been nice, for instance, if he'd offered to drive her around today instead of breezing on off up to Palmdale to some drag meeting with the other kids. Of course, racing was important to him—she struggled to be loyal about it. But a fellow ought to care enough about his girl to help out in a spot like this. He kept saying, "Don't worry," until she wanted to scream. He should just inquire once about the rent on a little apartment—anything in a good neighborhood.

The bus came and Christie got on, grabbed one of the few remaining seats, and gratefully eased her aching arches loose in the high-heeled pumps. Inadvertently she looked up to meet her own eyes in the mirror above the door of the bus. It jiggled with the vibration, made her look blurred and jittery. At the next stop, though, it quieted down—Christie questioned it anxiously. A funny little face, damp with perspiration, blond hair hanging limp, eyes wide and accusing: Who'd marry you? The secret whisper came to catch her sharply, like an old familiar pain.

15

She hoped the folks wouldn't be home. They almost never were on a Saturday, and today especially Christie didn't feel like answering a lot of questions. But luck wasn't with her. The old patterns were crumbling; instead of Dad's spending the day at the shop, going over the account books as he usually did, she found him there in the living room, sitting at the desk writing letters. As she let herself into the apartment, he looked up smiling.

"Hi, toots." A big hearty man, he had this irritating way of spouting ancient slang as though that somehow put him on an even basis with her and the other kids.

Christie said, "Hi, Dad," and headed for her room.

"Been downtown? I'll bet it was hot." As usual he kept talking so that she had to stop or else be impolite. "Heat nearly conked me out, too. I worked on the trailer all morning—put up some shelves. Here, hon, sit down and take it easy. How's if I stir us up a batch of lemonade?"

"No, thanks." Christie knew it sounded unfriendly, but he really shouldn't expect to buy her happiness with a pitcher of lemonade.

"Well, it sure will seem great to be headed out of this old smudge pot of a city," he went on bluffly, but behind the beaming front there was a look of misery, too. Christie felt a moment of encouragement, a faint glimmer of compatibility. Sitting down in front of the fan, she kicked off her shoes.

"Dad," she said earnestly, "would you think it was just terrible if I stayed home? Not here—I know this

16

apartment costs a lot. But I could get a room somewhere and finish school. I mean, don't you think school's important?"

He glanced away. She could tell, by the poker-faced look, that he was trying to decide on a good answer, not a straightforward one.

"Well, now," he said, "I had an idea you'd be glad to get rid of the old 'drag.'"

"Just because I don't especially like school," she said carefully, still trying to get to him for once on even terms, "that doesn't mean I oughtn't to stay here and finish. Just like you've always said, a high-school diploma is a necessity these days."

"Oh, I agree," he answered gravely. "And I do hope you'll finish. I just think a short interim period won't necessarily hurt you. Might lend perspective to all sorts of things. Of course I'm sorry I had to bolix you socially by taking you away from your friends just now, with senior-year activities coming up. But then we can't always help things like that—life's full of surprises."

A swift suspicion crossed Christie's mind—there was something about the way he said it that didn't ring quite true. She knew that Dad didn't care much for Rudy, but he certainly wouldn't tear up their whole home on that account! It wasn't even thinkable. No, he really was sick, she told herself firmly, and she must be as tolerant as possible. This shrugging off the idea of school was probably part of his illness.

17

Patiently she said, "But, Dad, wouldn't you trust me to live in a nice place like the YWCA?"

"Kit, I do trust you—" He really was looking pretty ill now, the thin strands of blond hair plastered wetly across his balding head. "I just think you ought to be with us. I mean, that we all ought to be together. This is a—it's going to be—interesting." The smile was pasted on loosely now.

"Sure, Dad." She sighed. "I guess it's going to be great." Be brave, carry on, and don't *ever* expect parents to understand.

Leaving her father to his letter writing, Christie got out of her clothes and took a long, cold shower. In the distance she heard a door bang and a high-pitched voice —when Mom came home you always knew it. She wasn't exactly loud, just constantly in a twitter. If they got to living in a space eight feet by twenty-four it was going to sound like the birdcage at the zoo. Not that Christie would be around by then—

When she came into the living room, comfortable in shorts and sandals, she found her mother still going on —all about the party they'd given for her at the Garden Club.

"They were so sweet—they said I was the best program chairman they ever had!" Mom was a small dark-haired woman with large brown eyes that seemed constantly stretched wide with wonder over everything. Happy wonder, angry wonder, but always the fine-penciled brows were lifted, the little mouth somewhere

18

between an "oo" and an "ah." She was rattling along to Dad, who wasn't half listening—you just couldn't listen to everything Mom said. When she saw Christie, she started in all over again.

"Kitty, dear, look—just *look* what the Garden Club gave me!"

It was an African violet, of course. Violets were Mom's puny passport into the club, because she didn't have a real garden, never had had one. Just planters full of African violets all over the place. She read about them and gave papers on them. Sometimes Christie had reflected that her mother would have loved her more if she'd grown in a pot.

Now she just felt a distant wonder at the thought of leaving them. Even parents are a way of life, and learning to live alone was going to be disturbing at first. After this perpetual hubbub, a single silent room was going to afford something more acute than privacy.

But it was going to be wonderful! Christie put her doubts aside firmly. To be independent, just to come and go as you please.

"I believe I'll take a little walk before dinner," she announced, already getting the feel of this self-assertion.

But Mom hardly paid attention, and Dad only noticed enough to hand her a bunch of letters. "Will you drop these in the mailbox for me, hon? Thanks."

Outside, the haze was still thick; the sun had given up trying and left just a smoldering red glow behind the folds of smog. What a crazy place to live, she thought.

19

And yet the swarming sound of the city around her was like the beat of her own pulse. It was all she'd known since she could remember. Without it, Christie thought, she'd probably die, little by little.

For a few blocks she walked along fast; when she spotted a mailbox across the street, she started to step off the curb, checked just in time as a car came screaming out of nowhere. The rush of air rocked her as it whipped past. A slick-looking car—Christie stared after it longingly. And then she glanced down and realized that when she'd jumped back, one of the letters had got away from her; tumbled along by the car, it had come to rest in the gutter. Unhappily she retrieved it to find a dirty tire tread printed across the face. Even though it was just to Aunt Nadine, she knew Dad wouldn't want to send it out that way. And yet to go all the way home—? Easier just to cut across to the corner drugstore.

She bought a package of envelopes and a stamp from the machine on the counter, then retreating to a deserted spot back near the phone booth, tore off the old envelope and was about to insert the letter in the clean one when a line stood out at her as if it had been written in neon, instead of Dad's black, square pen strokes.

Christie doesn't know how serious her condition is.

She stood staring at the page, no longer conscious of where she was or what she was doing, reading a letter not meant for her. As detached as if she were alone in time and space, Christie read on:

20

The doctor says she is in a state of high nervous tension. This black-out in class a while back was a safety valve, it warded off a more serious crisis. But she is stripping her gears trying to keep up a hectic pace. There must be other reasons—hidden frustrations that she hasn't confided to us. But we can't pry them out of her, of course. We can't even tell her how close she is to becoming really ill. The doctor is sure this will react in exactly the wrong way —increase the strain she is under.

He doesn't believe psychiatry is necessary or advisable at this point. He is sure that a good deal of the trouble lies in her generally poor physical condition, which is not being helped by the foul atmosphere of the city. So we are going to attack the problem on that front first, take her to some place where she'll be forced to get plenty of rest, sun, and no tensions for a few months.

The story is that we're going on my account— remember that when you write. I've sold the shop; it hasn't been showing profit lately, just a matter of time before I'd have had to close up. So I salvaged what I could, but frankly it didn't bring much; we're going to have to keep to a tight budget for the immediate future. That's why I decided, after a certain amount of study, that the cheapest way to manage was to buy a used house trailer. . . .

Christie folded the letter; in a daze she put it in an envelope and addressed it. Moving mechanically, she mailed the letters and started back slowly toward the apartment, clenched in the grip of sudden comprehension.

21

So this was all for her. . . . Mom and Dad were a couple of people stuck with an unraveling kid, people who did understand, after all. And Rudy? He was part of the beautiful world that didn't care, that would go right on rolling after Christie Ford had faded off into the desert to try to get her nerves strung back together. Rudy was just a voice somewhere in the past. . . . "You're the only thing that ever gets me off the ground."

What a laugh.

3

On the map, the desert is a big blank area where towns are only far-flung white dots connected by a few thin lines. To head out into it, Christie thought bleakly, was a little like venturing into a hostile foreign land. The long reaches of gray sand stretched off until they became one with the gray sky. As suddenly as the dropping of a veil, autumn had come down upon them. A chilly small rain was falling steadily, turning the details knife-edge sharp. Occasional fields of black volcanic rock glistened harshly in the wet. The stunted trees that grew in the draws were strung with dripping thorns, and the spines of the barrel cactus had turned bright crimson, lending a rare savage smattering of color to the monotonous wasteland.

Ahead of them, the highway glistened, straight as a steel tape and almost as slick, to judge by the anxious concentration with which Sam Ford handled the car. He always did drive as if he were anchored down, and now, of course, there was the trailer lumbering along behind like some big bull-nosed silvery fish on a stringer.

Bunched down in the corner of the back seat, Christie looked over her shoulder at the thing. One of Mom's planters was firmly stashed in a holder in the front window. Christie felt an impulse to giggle mirthlessly. How crazy can you get, to have an African violet trundling along behind you?

And then she went all soft inside, as she thought for the thousandth time how these two were slicing themselves loose from everything they were used to, their work and friends. Stella Ford . . . such a charming woman . . . so active. And Sam Ford . . . nice guy . . . good mixer . . . very civic-minded. Christie had heard them described in just about those words time and again. She herself had just taken them for granted: So you have parents. Now it was strange to think of them as people —people who could be, even, frightened.

When Dad turned to glance back at the trailer, she saw signs of it in his eyes. It had been coming on ever since he'd turned over the keys of the furniture shop to somebody else. Mom, too—plump little hands squeezed tight in her lap—she must be scared rigid, Christie thought. Her whole life had been geared to hovering over centerpieces. What on earth would she do without somebody to discuss flowers with or compare notes?

Just to know that they were so human made Christie ache to reach out and help them—at least to clear the air of secrets. But she couldn't, not so long as they couldn't. All through the dreary chore of packing they had played their little game, Dad talking about his "doctor's orders" and Mom just talking . . . talking. . . .

Christie had tried to maintain a gloss of cheerfulness, but it had left her emotionally exhausted. Worst of all were the nights, when she lay still and awake, trying to imagine—then trying to stop imagining. The long, sleepless hours had left her tense with weariness. Now that they were on their way, she felt the stiffening go out of her. Nothing to do but lean back and wait for—what?

"The filling-station man said about twenty-five miles," Mom remarked in muted tones. "We've gone twenty-seven already."

"I know," Dad muttered, peering at the horizon.

There didn't seem to be anything out there. They had long since left civilization behind—Palm Springs, Salton Sea, all the gay places where there might have been a nice spot, even with a swimming pool. Christie reminded herself that any such luxuries would have been expensive. But since leaving the resort areas most of the villages they had passed were just little scrabbles of houses without even an attempt at a trailer court.

They had finally found one in which to spend last night and had no sooner got parked than they were surrounded by an army of smeary children, with fringes

25

of gawking older folk, listless men and uncorseted women. The Fords had turned in early, slept poorly, and got up at daybreak to go on with their search.

"I see something ahead," Dad said, "but it doesn't exactly look like a trailer park."

As they drove nearer, a double pair of railroad tracks curved in to parallel the highway, as if they, too, were searching for the little junction, where some drab buildings squatted together under a single old salt cedar. They seemed to be crowding each other for shelter, afraid to stand out in the open against this huge, silent country—just a frame filling station and a small adobe house, behind which a few trailers were parked on an area that had been scraped clear of black rock. Dad slowed the car, studying the situation.

Silently Christie prayed—oh, no! Not here! At least a town of some sort where there'd be a movie house, a few stores. What do these people do all day? And the answer came back like mockery: They rest. In the peace and quiet, they rest. She bit down on her lip and kept still as Dad steered on into the station.

The sign in front of the pumps read: THE OASIS. Gas —Oil—Eats—Drinks—Ice. Wayne Slater, Prop. A man in his young thirties was putting gas in another car.

"Be right with you," he called across in a nervous tone that meant: Please don't go away, I need the business.

Ford pulled up far enough to get a good look at the court. The grounds were neat—not like the place last night which had been a shambles of unassorted junk.

26

The two trailers nearest the highway looked permanent, each with its shed in back, its faded awning sagging a little with rain water just now. They'd obviously been here so long they had taken root. Beyond them loomed a huge red-and-black job, as big and as ugly as a boxcar. It was fairly well entrenched, but looked movable; there was a green pickup parked in front of it. Opposite these three stood two older trailers, dog-eared and drab. No awnings or little rows of stones to set off the boundaries of their patios. Christie thought they must be recent arrivals, though it hardly seemed possible that the dilapidated cars parked in front could have pulled them over the road. They stood isolated, as if more than peeling paint separated them from the rest of the court. Two men were out in the rain, struggling to pull a tarpaulin over the top of one.

Uneasily, Dad murmured, "This isn't exactly what I'd pictured for us. . . ."

"Well, pet," Mom said with tremulous brightness, "we didn't come out here to socialize." Her tone was seasoned with meaning that Christie understood perfectly.

Now a girl had come to stand in the door of the filling station, staring blankly at their trailer, her face slack, one hand absently feeling the mat of pin curls that bristled from her head. She couldn't have been more than twenty-five, but her face was already set in a twist of defeat. And why not? Christie thought. Stuck out here, that's how I'll get, too, in a month or so.

27

The man came hustling over at last. "Fill her up?"

"I'm looking for trailer space for the winter," Dad told him. "Something nice and quiet with modern facilities."

"You mean a plumbing hookup? I got that—I got a good big septic tank. I got water, too, I got a deep well." The man was painfully eager, his long, homely face molded in an expression of anxiety that the smile didn't erase.

"Electricity?" Ford asked.

"Well, I got a little power plant, enough to run the pumps and the big refrigerator inside. I get fresh meat and vegetables once a week delivered from the city, milk and all that. My wife, Mabel, runs a store for the folks here. Only my plant don't make enough juice to carry a load of trailers with all them appliances. But then that makes it quiet—real quiet. We got no loud TV's going —" Any minute, Christie thought, he might lie down and make like a rug.

"What does one do for light?" her mother asked.

"Most folks got gasoline lanterns. And I sell ice; you can put a chunk in your refrig, keeps things good. Everybody makes out okay. We had a lot of people, no complaints. Up to last week we had a whole construction crew in here, only the road job got done, so they pulled out, except for the guy in the big trailer. Him and his wife figure to sit out the winter here. It's only fifteen bucks a month and you can't live that cheap hardly nowhere."

28

Mom was going on asking about the mail delivery, where the nearest telephone was; but Christie saw the decision already coming in Dad's face.

Nodding grimly, he said, "I think this will do."

They chose the hookup farthest away from the highway. Dad said it was for more peace and quiet, but Christie thought privately it was to give himself plenty of room to back in. After three tries, all he had managed to do was jackknife the trailer. In trying to straighten it, he jockeyed himself in tighter against the line of boulders that formed the boundary of the cleared area, and finally wound up with his front tire jammed against a huge chunk of the black rock, while the back of the trailer teetered out precariously over a gulch that ran along the margin of the court.

Christie looked up into the weeping skies and consigned herself to being plunged in the ditch.

Ford got out to study the situation, his light flannels beginning at once to speckle in the rain, setting Mom off into little incoherent phrases about raincoats and umbrellas. Staring philosophically out the window, Christie noticed that the two men had climbed off the top of the threadbare trailer and were coming over.

One of them was short and stocky, dressed in an old slicker. Under the brim of the fraying straw hat his face was dark brown and ageless as only a Mexican's can be. The other was tall, fair-skinned, and younger. Hard to tell how old he was. Beneath the clinging, wet shirt sleeves his body was molded hard, but the broad, clean-cut face was youthful. There was something about him that pricked Christie keenly—the way he followed the Mexican by three or four steps almost blindly, the blank containment of his face, as if, like herself, he was braced against some sort of inner pressure.

She waited for him to glance up and see her, but he just stood with his look stopping short somewhere around the front bumper of the car. It was the Mexican who spoke.

"Not so easy, parking the trailer," he said shyly. "I think maybe—could we help?"

"Thank you, sir." Dad shook hands sheepishly. "I'm afraid I've got her stymied. Looks like it'll take a couple of crowbars to loosen that rock."

"What you think, Joel?" The Mexican raised his voice in slight insistence.

Rousing, the boy looked at the rock, went over and laid hold of it. Christie saw the muscles tense in his arms below the rolled-up sleeves. He set his hands in a new position and threw more weight into the effort—the stone broke loose and he wheeled it aside almost carelessly.

Dad's jaw came ajar. "Good work!"

Joel ducked his head in acknowledgment, but there still wasn't much response in his look.

It was the Mexican who stood out in front and motioned with neat circling gestures to guide Dad out of their tight spot. Still watching the boy, Christie felt a more insistent prodding of curiosity. He couldn't be much older than she was and yet he moved with all the beautiful coordination of a man. Even in the way he stood there was a graceful, loose-jointed poise that she'd seen only in good athletes.

As if her interest had finally pulled him out of his cell of concentration, Joel looked up. The vivid, wind-struck, blue eyes met hers with an unwavering aware-ness.

Christie smiled—it started out as an automatic gesture but warmed into a wordless greeting. She saw it take effect on him, although he didn't return it—just stared at her with a silent communication that fluttered her in-wardly. It was she who finally let her look fall in con-fusion.

With the trailer parked, Mom was inviting them all in for coffee. But the Mexican—Pete Moreno, he said his name was—shook his head.

"Thank you, but we must go back. My old box, she's got a leak." He touched the brim of his hat, then turned to the boy. "You coming, Joel?" he asked gently. The young man moved over to his side, and the two of them walked back together. Irritably, Christie was glad to see them go. To be looked at so—so thoughtfully—! It wasn't even complimentary.

Leaving Dad to study the complexities of unhitching, she followed her mother into the shadowy depths of the trailer.

"I think I have some candles somewhere." Mom had

31

begun to talk again, as if in damp determination to drown out all undertones of misgiving. "Isn't this fun, Kitty? I feel like a pioneer."

Christie mumbled something. Pioneer, hah. The pioneers had some place to go; they were always on their way somewhere to do important things like found cities or discover rivers or something. At least there were dangers to be met. She could imagine what the pioneers would think of squatting on a two-by-four plot of sand rented from a filling station, spending their lives crouched inside a metal box. Glancing out the window of her bedroom, Christie saw that the view was graced by a lovely old dead bush. If the pioneers didn't like the view, there was plenty of room in those days to move on. But she didn't mention it. Mom was still back there in the front room, going on about the good old covered-wagon spirit. Her voice seemed louder than usual.

Christie tried to summon up all the tolerance she was capable of, reminding herself again of the towering obligation she was under to her parents. It was an uncomfortable sensation, to be the cause of all this. Duty was beginning to be a dirty word. She had to sympathize with them, they must be secretly exasperated to death! But understanding it didn't cure it. She could hear the discord already beginning to jangle. And when the nothingness and boredom had time to drill in, Christie knew that the desert was going to bring out the worst in everybody. She could feel it coming on.

4

Next morning the rain was still drumming away on the roof of the Tin Trap, as Christie had privately dubbed their home on wheels. There was still no light; the candles had all burned down the evening before, even though they had gone to bed at the unearthly hour of nine o'clock. It was clammy cold again, too. The heater ran on oil, of which they had none. Dad had assured them that the desert was going to be deliciously balmy all winter.

So the three of them sat in medium gloom, grouped in front of the gas stove. The kitchen was just a state of mind set off from the living room by a waist-high divider, so it didn't hold the warmth very well. There

33

wasn't even a good cup of black coffee to drive off the inner chill; Dad had been "taken off" coffee by the doctor. Christie stared at her cup of hot chocolate and wondered if she was going to be able to get any of the sticky, sweet stuff down.

This morning it seemed to be choking Dad a little, too. He glanced at the toast that Mom had fried in the skillet and shoved away from the table.

"I'd better get going. I may have to drive halfway back to L. A. to find gasoline lanterns."

A curious, panicky thought brushed Christie's mind —without the car, they wouldn't even have a radio, no way to be in touch with the world—as lost as if they were on the face of the moon!

In the bustle of Dad's departure she managed to escape the rest of breakfast, taking refuge in her room where she could stop trying to look bright. She felt as useless as a half pair of scissors.

Rain pelted against the metal so near overhead that she could almost feel the burst of the drops. She stood at the window watching it course down the side of the trailer, making little pools that overflowed into bigger pools. With irresistible stubbornness it ate channels—one trickle joining another, fingering out new ways to get across the court and into the big wash, where a good-sized stream was flowing. Stupid water, absolutely bent on getting somewhere, doing something; must have an ambition to be a flood.

This is frantic! Christie swallowed hard against the

34

pounding in her throat. Feverishly she began to dress, choosing the brightest colors in the closet. The blue angora sweater felt warm and hid her skimpiness—she always felt better when she wore it. The new heather wool skirt was flattering, too. Defiantly she brushed her hair hard until it shone. Put on lipstick. No need for eye shadow, that was for sure!

Going up to the front of the trailer, she found her mother dusting busily. Stella looked over her shoulder and smiled with visible determination.

"Don't you look nice, Kitty!" she chirped. "Come help me set out my violets. I'm so glad I have plenty of shelves." So Dad's carpentry was paying off. Maybe that's why they got married, Christie thought dryly: Dad was a shelf man and Mom had always been the knickknack type—grinning china fish, glass swans, vases, ash trays.

"I thought I'd go to the store and see if they have any magazines," she said evasively. "Anything you want?"

"Well, that's sweet of you. Yes, we do need butter. And milk and bread—get some lettuce if they have it. Whatever looks good to you, dear. Take my purse. And take the umbrella."

Quickly Christie scooped up her mother's wallet and plucked the umbrella from the narrow closet next to the refrigerator, slipped on out before Mom could think of a dozen other precautions. It was getting a little nerve-racking. . . .

35

She bit down hard on that thought. I am *not* nervous. I am calm, like a cup of custard. But her hands clenched tight on the umbrella as she started down the court.

Glancing over at the two shabby trailers that stood opposite the others, she was glad to let her mind dart out in a different direction. What would Pete Moreno be doing on a day like this, behind the burlap curtains drawn across his windows? More especially, what about this Joel? The trailer next to the Mexican's was dark, the windows bare of hangings; what could the boy and his parents be doing in there without light or movement? Sleeping, probably. Some people could sleep half their lives away. But Joel hardly looked the type.

Maybe it accounted for his strangeness; being cooped up here in outer space with nothing to spend his energy on, not even a town closer than thirty miles. And yet, presumably he was old enough to go and live his own life. There hadn't been anything kiddish about the way he'd studied her yesterday. Other men—boys like Rudy —never meet your eyes as steadily as that. When she reached the filling station and stepped in under the canopy, Christie found Wayne Slater rushing around in a panic with three customers all needing attention at once. She said a small "hello," but he looked right through her, ran over to get a quart of oil, and stabbed it with the opener as if it were some mortal enemy.

Closing the umbrella, Christie went on into the room that served both as restaurant and store. It was a hectic little cubbyhole; between the short-order counter on one

36

side and the grocery counter on the other was stacked an assortment of odds and ends, souvenirs, auto accessories, post cards—everything, apparently, that Slater had ever had a request for.

Perched on a stool beside the cash register was the discontented girl in pin curls—Christie supposed this was Mabel—languidly applying polish to her nails. As the door whined shut, she looked up, took in the blue sweater and blond hair, and began to detest Christie. With a purposeful rudeness that was positively stimulating she went back to dabbing on the Savage Scarlet.

Christie felt better than she had in days. Most girls, if they ever did feel a twinge of jealousy, were careful to hide it. Coolly she waited. Not for anything would she have spoiled the effect by seeming impatient.

The silence seemed to be working against Mabel. She squirmed, spoiled one of her nails, angrily took the polish off, and was about to begin all over when the screen creaked again and Pete Moreno stepped in, his slicker shedding water. Still following on his heels came Joel.

As they walked over to the counter, the Mexican touched his hat to Christie. She was starting to say something polite when suddenly Mabel became available. Rushing up with her claws still wet, she greeted the men with raucous warmth.

"Hi, Joey. Pedro, how's everything? How's the baby's cold?"

"Not so good," the Mexican said soberly. "She been crying. I need a can of milk, please."

Christie had stepped aside to make room. Now she kept on going, clear on over to the magazines, trying not to show the pinch of being an outsider to their conversation. The only safe thing in sight was a month-old copy of *Vogue*. It seemed pretty fruitless to torment herself with that kind of reading matter out here, but she tucked it under her arm and went back to the counter.

The Mexican had gone out again, but Joel lingered behind, engrossed in a newspaper he had picked up from the stand.

"What's new, Joey?" Mabel was asking, all sugar. "Does it say in the paper all what you should wear when you come live in a trailer camp these days?"

Christie got the drift and couldn't quite suppress a smile as she laid the copy of *Vogue* on the counter and got out her purse.

"Of course, you and me aren't the ee-lite, Joey. We don't stick up our snoots when a sweet guy like Pete comes around, so what if he is a Mexican? But then some people think they're the whole country club—or didn't you notice how one trailer's parked all off by itself at the end of the court? Joey, you're not listening!"

Christie had stiffened inwardly. This was a good deal worse than cattiness; this kind of malice was as corrosive as lye. She glanced at the boy. He was still scanning the paper.

Mabel made one more try. "Well, maybe I ain't the *Vogue* type, but then I work for a living. What can I do for you, Joey?"

38

Folding the newssheet, he laid it on the counter. "You can go ahead and serve the lady," he said, in a deep, quiet voice.

With a small start of gratification Christie murmured, "Thank you." And to the woman, "I'd like to buy a loaf of bread and a quart of fresh milk."

Mabel reeled off a laugh. "I got news for you, girly. Friday is 'fresh' day and this is only Wednesday, which means the milk has run out, likewise the bread and the vegetables. And we don't carry no little tidbits like pheasant under glass."

Abruptly Christie flared with disgust. When it came to cutting remarks this stupid creature's blowtorch wasn't even lit. Tartly she commented, "If it gets any fresher in here on Friday, you can grow your own cat-nip. I'll take a can of vegetable soup and a box of crackers, please."

In a thick silence she paid and left.

Out in the rain again, Christie welcomed the sting of the drops on her face. As hot as if she'd just come out of a phone booth, she looked up into the falling skies and wondered why this sickly little clash had come about. Why couldn't the woman be civilized and hate her in silence?

It was raining hard enough to soak the bag of groceries; Christie went about opening the umbrella. For a second it stuck. And then Joel came up beside her, took it, and raised it with delicate persuasion, handing it back to her gravely.

39

"That's the second time you've come to my rescue," she thanked him lightly. "I guess we ought to get acquainted. I know your name is Joel. I'm Kit Ford."

"Kit?" he repeated. Again the low pitch of his voice struck a pleasant vibration through her. As he matched his step to hers, Christie felt small and feminine, even a little excited.

"Maybe I'm not tuned in," she was chatting breezily, "but all that silly business in the store escapes me. Why are the flags flying upside down?"

Joel shot her a questioning look, then shrugged. "Don't mind Mable. She's that way with everybody. The desert's hard on some people," he added, the brittle blue eyes fixed on the faint profile of rock cliffs that rose dimly in the distance, putting a horizon around the empty desert.

"But—to accuse somebody of up-snootery! Well, with me that goes down in lumps!" she insisted.

Joel nodded absently. "Why waste time thinking about her?"

"Thinking isn't exactly my dish of fish. I just bounce when I'm hit—it's automatic." And then feeling as if the line was loaded with sinkers, Christie tried a new approach. "Hey, aren't you getting damp? How about ducking under the tent?"

Joel blinked the drops off his lashes. "Thanks, but it's nothing to me whether I get wet. Something about rain" —he seemed to search for words—"it's kinder than sun."

40

"Well, I agree! The only reason I carry this thing is because if I sneeze my mother catches cold. You know parents—" She faltered a little as those blue eyes swung around and almost scorched her. Laughing insistently, she said, "I mean they're the craziest, when it comes to worrying about the offspring. If they'd just leave us alone . . ." *Oh murder, what did I say?* She quivered inside at the growing intensity of his look.

Explosively he snapped, "Do you really think it's so wonderful to be left alone?" Then, as if regretting the burst of violence, he shook his head. "I'm sorry. You'll excuse me?" And turning, he went into the gray trailer next to the Mexican's. The door closed behind him quietly.

Christie stood stunned a minute before she moved on, lost in a whole terrible swarm of thoughts. That harmless crack about parents had brought him out like a switch-blade knife. And his answer could mean only one thing. As she walked on slowly, she glanced back, but still no light showed in those uncurtained windows.

Wrinkling with remorse, Christie trudged on home. When she gave the sack of groceries to her mother, she dropped a clumsy, guilty little kiss on the powdery cheek. Mom looked shocked, which made Christie feel ten times worse. Taking refuge in the privacy of her own room, she sank down on the bed weakly, her mind a haze of conflict.

Ever since she'd read that phrase in Dad's letter about having hidden frustrations, she'd been wondering what secret misery she must be harboring that she wasn't even aware of. She wished she'd read more of those columns that fill you in on your symptoms, because she was beginning to think her trouble all came from a bad case of no-personality. Even what little she'd been able to acquire seemed to get continually pulled out from under her. Hard as she tried, there were these awful stumbles —some people she just couldn't get with. It had happened before. Though why this, today, should seem worse—?

From far off she heard a train whistle—the saddest sound in the world. It came on slowly, the pulsing of the big diesels heavy enough to shake the ground. Ponderously they passed, hauling a line of clackety cars, heading west for Los Angeles.

And Christie cried.

5

"What I don't understand," remarked Sam Ford, "is why on the immortal earth, with thousands of acres to choose from, did anyone build right here beside the railroad tracks?"

"That's easy." Everything was easy to Al McKinney, the construction worker. A fleshy man in his forties, he was an "easy" type: dressed in loose-fitting comfortable clothes with a western flair of style and color; bland, good-natured features; his manner, too, was loose and pleasant. "This used to be a watering stop for the old chug-chugs. The well was already in, so naturally that made it a setup for a station. Ought to be a gold mine, but that poor jerk Slater don't know how to shoot the

43

angles. He's too busy sweatin'."

Christie, standing with them under the awning which Dad had just erected, saw her father wince at the bluntness of McKinney's language, but she didn't have the energy to be amused. This sun wasn't actually as hot as in Los Angeles, but the brutal brightness was enough to make a person shrink three sizes. Or maybe, she thought, she still felt shriveled from that crying spell yesterday. She tried to forget that and focus on what the men were saying.

"To run one's own business," Dad was pontificating, "requires a certain amount of—sweat."

"Aanh—" McKinney made an inarticulate, skeptical noise. "It's the guys with the angles that rake in cash. I told him, put up some signs, put a girl on 'em, get a slogan like 'Slater's Greater.' Or go catch a gila monster, advertise you got a zoo. At least he ought to fix the grounds up, slop some paint on those rocks out front. Women go for a nice-looking place. And as far as the trailer park's concerned, if he wants to drag in the overnighters, he better throw out the trash."

"I've been wondering who occupied the spaces up in front," Ford remarked curiously. "Seems strange that anyone would want to live here permanently."

"Aanh"—McKinney shrugged—"couple of pensioners. Can't afford nothing fancier than this. They're harmless. Except Slater ought to put 'em back here away from the road, save the front spots for good-looking rigs like yours and mine. But man, he's begging for real

44

trouble when he lets those Okies hang around."

Following his look to the two trailers opposite, Ford said on a sharp note of surprise, "You mean those people are migrant workers?"

"Right. They're pickers, and pickers are germs. They're all carrying gray dodgers. Steal you bald-headed. I'd like to see the collection of swiped tools that wetback must have hid away in his old pigeon coop. Before the work crew left, they was ready to lynch him."

Mildly Ford changed the subject. "How is it that you happened to stay on, Mac?"

"Easy. It's cheap here. Won't be any road work until February or March, after the contracts get let. I got friends in the San Berdoo union office; they'll keep my name alive on the list. I might as well relax. Desert don't bother me like it does some."

Christie stared out across the vast lake of sand, broken only by the outcroppings of black rock that thrust up through it like the remnants of prehistoric craters. Aglint with the merciless white sunlight, it was as frightening as any piece of earth she had ever imagined. And the quiet—the big quiet that ate up all the feeble human noises—that was the most unnerving of all. It was like a judgment. It made Christie want to yell or blaze away on a good loud auto horn—anything to prove that noise could still top all this silence.

Now from far out across the distances the fitful, two-toned cry of a diesel whistle came thinly; even it seemed to be on the verge of getting lost in the enveloping hush

45

of the land. Leaving the two men to their gabbing, Christie stepped out under the downbeat of the sun and headed for the front of the court.

For all that the trains goaded her with homesick longing, they were a relief, too—the one moment of sound and action breaking the static hours. Mostly freights, they came through several times a day, the ones from Los Angeles barreling along fast, the westbound trains moving more slowly, as if there must be a slight imperceptible tilt to the flat country, causing them to labor harder. This one was creeping more slowly than usual. Christie could hear the engines' huge pulse throbbing, as if they, too, were straining under a knot of nerves.

Hurrying a little, she passed the old men who had come out, like ancient rabbits, to sit in the sun. Something about the sight of them, teetering idly in the folding chairs, watching her with their old eyes the color of weathered boards, almost unstrung her. They looked as helpless as prisoners serving out a life sentence. *Who wants to live that long?*

Almost running, she reached the tracks as the freight came plugging slowly toward the crossing. *I must be getting whirly,* she told herself with a touch of scorn. *Trotting out to watch a train like some little shanty-town girl—!*

The diesels ground past, as impersonal as if they were remote-controlled. Nobody standing at the window to wave, no hot coals spitting out a funnel on top. But the cars themselves still made that wonderful shuffling sound and bore the magic names of far-flung places . . . Wabash . . . Northern Pacific . . . Bangor and Aroostook . . . Lackawanna . . . Grand Trunk Western . . . Rock Island Rocket . . . Mainline of Mid-America. . . .

And a man looked down at her from that one. He was riding the ladder, hanging to it carelessly with one hand; in the other he carried a bedroll. Because he was there, moving past, bound to be gone in another minute, Christie stared at him without self-consciousness.

A strange sort of man. No trainman, that was sure. Not young, but not old, either. Under the sun his hair was bright rust color, rumpled. A stubble of beard labeled him a tramp, but the keen alertness of his face denied it. When his eyes met hers for a minute, Christie was struck by swift curiosity. She thought he could be a master criminal or a priest. Or a jester.

He was past her now, scanning the crossroads community. Then to her infinite shock he tossed the bedroll down and swung off the train lightly, stumbled with the momentum but recovered, as if he'd done it many times before.

Christie was already retreating, taking a long circular course to circumvent him. She was suddenly afraid. He watched her go, for a minute stood there dusting the bedroll off absently, then slung it over his shoulder and headed for the station.

"Yeah, sure, he hopped off that freighter yesterday, but he's no bum." Wayne Slater spoke in a lowered voice.

47

"What makes you say so?" asked Sam Ford. "The glimpse I had of him, he looked like any other hobo."

Christie, stretched out in a folding chair not far from where the men were standing, had to listen intently to catch the words. She didn't want to seem too interested, but when Slater had come over to the trailer this morning and called McKinney to join them, she'd had an idea it was about the redheaded man.

McKinney was holding forth indignantly now. "A bindle stiff is a bindle stiff. They're all carrying gray dodgers."

Slater shook his head. "Not this guy. He's clean, and he talks good. He talks kinda crazy, but he uses four-dollar words. I figure maybe he's, like they say, a radical or something." His voice had dropped almost to a whisper.

"You wouldn't—" Dad sounded uneasy. "Would you let a drifter hang around?"

"Well, he didn't ask for a handout," Slater said grudgingly. "He's willing to work. And what gets me, he's a real hot-shot mechanic and no fooling. I had a Caddie pull in this morning, carburetor trouble—she was shaking like a leaf. You should have seen this guy calm her down. He's got hands like a doctor. Man, could I use a good grease monkey! Only catch is—"

"Catch is," supplied McKinney, "he wants your shirt and your right arm."

"Nah. That's what I don't get. He don't want any pay. All he wants is to bunk down in the station and—"

48

"Got his eye on your cash register." McKinney grinned.

"I keep my cash on me," snapped Slater. "He says he'll take some food and a place to sleep and make the rest on tips. He's got this theory: All I do is let him price his own time, he gives the customer a twenty-dollar job and only charges ten, so the customer tips him good and I make ten bucks. I don't have to figure out any withholding tax from his wages because he don't make any wages. It's cockeyed but it makes sense, you know what I mean? What sold me is that about how I get out of all the withholding bunko."

"You get out of it and he gets out of it," Ford said.

"That's his business. Me, I'm not nobody's keeper, and you don't know what a bind you can get in. I got sales taxes, gas taxes, income tax—even I got food tax to figure. I tell you I'm tax-pooped."

"Then what's the catch?" McKinney asked.

"The catch is, I don't know what the catch is," Slater said soberly. "Burnett's got some angle, like you say. I asked him why he skipped that train here, and he give me a pitch about how he slept through Arizona and forgot to get off there. It was a runaround if I ever heard one. Except who am I to care why the guy picked this place? If I'm making money?"

"Then you're actually going to take him on?" Dad was sounding more worried by the minute, Christie thought.

"Mr. Ford, I can't turn him down. I don't like it,

49

myself, but it's a chance to get even on my books. I just wanted you all to know what the score was, and I told him he can't come snooping back here. He's got to stay out front and keep his nose clean or he gets the boot."

"I'd feel a little more comfortable if we knew why he didn't decide to take a train back to Arizona," Ford said slowly.

"Me, too. I asked him, what the Sam Hill you want to stay here for? You know what he says? He says, 'There's a time to gather stones together.'" Slater looked at them helplessly. "Nuts. Just nuts."

6

All that day and the next, Christie kept close to the trailer. She found excuses not to go to the store, didn't even lounge around outside. Closeted—and that was the word for it—in her own room, she tried to read, wrote long, rambling letters to everybody she could think of. Anything to drive off the utter deadliness of thinking, thinking.

Every time her thoughts slanted inward, she tried to shut them off, turn them to something else. Rudy—he seemed already so far in the past, part of another whole life. Joel—she hadn't seen him since that bad minute in front of his trailer. No memory to want to linger over. McKinney and the others were dull. Slater—Mabel—

Her own folks were dull and depressed. Right now, in the distance, she could hear Mom's voice going on almost as if she were trying to hammer back the silence with it.

How long can an afternoon get? Christie lay flat on her bed and eyed the ceiling.

So go on and think about Burnett. It gave her an odd qualm, but she knew she'd better face up to thinking about him. Nothing had happened since he'd come, no world-shaking events. He minded his own business, stayed in the garage most of the time, working on one car after another. But there was this feeling of something impending.

Once she had seen him walk out across the desert, seemingly at ease with his thorny surroundings. More than just at ease. He had blended with this brutal land as smoothly as a lean red fox. A keener nudge of uneasiness made Christie try to shut off this channel of speculation, too.

Squirming over onto her stomach, she saw that the late-afternoon sun was prying through the cracks of the Venetian blinds. Restlessly she got up to close them tighter; then, with her hand on the cord, it occurred to her that this was the worst subterfuge, trying to shut out the desert. Like trying to turn off Niagara Falls.

With abrupt, angry determination she yanked the blinds open and looked out. So it's just one million acres of land. Earth. After walking the dangerous canyons of the city, what is there to be afraid of in far horizons?

52

Chiding herself, to keep up her fortitude, Christie changed to dungarees, put on her sturdiest shoes and tied a kerchief over her head.

And yet when she did step out into the sheet of sunlight, she couldn't help faltering a little. The blinding clearness was really unfair. Eyes aren't made to look out so far or to see such vivid detail everywhere. With just a touch of compromise, she went down the bank into the big dry wash and decided to follow it a way, at least until she got used to being alone under the vast vault of sky.

Looking down, watching her footing, she was caught by the sight of a tracery of green. The bed of the gulch was bone-dry again, of course. Even the first day after the rain the temporary torrent had subsided, dwindling into puddles, and then even these had evaporated. But now, in the hollows, something beautiful—and hopeless —was happening. In the wake of that brief nourishment, a small growth was shoving upward—slender green stems, bent double, were trying to straighten into the cruel noonday sun.

As Christie began to walk slowly down the bottom of the wash, she was drawn from one spot to the next. They'll be sorry, she grieved, the poor lost little seeds, probably blown from some friendlier climate. They've picked a rough place to sprout.

A short way down the gully she crossed a set of small tracks; with her limited city knowledge, she decided they were a rabbit's. Rather a cruel thought, to picture what warm-blooded creatures must go through to survive this waterless place. And yet there were countless holes everywhere, some of them meticulously lined with the thorniest cactus needles—barrier against outside intrusion. Christie warmed toward the furry creatures. To hedge the world off with spiny spikes was a better solution than surrounding yourself with smiling pretense.

A new pattern on the floor of the gulch attracted her eye; at the edge of a mudhole she saw an imprint that made no sense—a series of small tracks left by something that had a row of snubby claws and practically no foot at all. In the softer spots the prints were a half-inch deep. She stood wondering over it—a gila monster?

From close above a small sound broke the quiet, no more than a sigh. Starting violently, Christie looked up into the imperturbable face that had glanced at her from the train. Burnett was sitting cross-legged on the bank of the wash, watching her. At close range his eyes were as clear as polished red agate. The stubble was shaven, the fine red hair combed, even the army surplus clothes looked in better press—and yet somehow he seemed more disturbing this way than hanging, disheveled, from a freight.

He sat quiet and spoke in a hushed voice. "I'm sorry I startled you. I guess I should have whistled something when I saw you coming along, but I'm not the whistling type."

Christie stood frozen, still suffering from the shock of his near presence.

54

"You're leery of me," he went on, much as he might try to soothe some frightened animal that was about to bolt. "I can't say I blame you. In fact, when I first spotted you standing beside the tracks, I was sure you were one of the sensitive ones. I almost kept on going, even though I had already decided to get off."

Christie was bringing herself under control now. There really was no reason to shake like this. So foolish—! She took a deep breath.

"I'm just—surprised," she told him unsteadily. "You —you don't expect to meet people out here."

Thoughtfully Burnett pulled an orange out of the pocket of his denim jacket and began to peel it, his long fingers moving adeptly. "And when you do, it's only common sense to give them a wide berth, just as you did the other day. That showed excellent judgment."

Christie laughed a little. She thought he must be joking, though he gave no evidence of it.

"I'm certainly not—not—I mean I can see no reason to—"

"To run away?" he helped her finish. "Well, take it from me, there's good reason, though not the sort that those unimaginative ones back yonder think. So now I've warned you and I won't again. Actually, it's quite gratifying to meet one of the Oasis-dwellers who is willing to share my dangerous society, at least momentarily. Something about my having disembarked from a train seems to hold them thunderstruck. Do you think it's so illogical? It's a very inexpensive way to travel."

55

Christie did laugh that time—he said it so seriously. She retorted, "What's not logical is choosing a place like this to stay, at the end of nowhere, when you could have gone on."

"Into Los Angeles?" He shook his head. "There's more to be said for the end of nowhere. Besides, it's an old stamping ground of mine."

"The desert is?"

"That's not what I meant," he said, with a quirk of humor that suddenly rendered his face unbelievably warm. "But, to be specific, I have been in the desert before—often enough to have learned some of its puzzles, if not all the answers. Every time I come into this ruthless country, I find a new flower."

Christie hesitated to take that personally, and yet the way he was smiling—

"Yes, that's what I meant," he assured her. "One of the tender, clean things of the earth that can be loved without stint." And then as some shading of suspicion must have shown in her face, his look sharpened. "You certainly don't mind being loved? Has our language become so warped that 'love' is only a crude, earthen word?"

Christie felt a blush coming, in spite of the detachment with which he was regarding her.

As if to himself, he went on. "I always wonder at the strength of young things. What an instinct to survive, and what faith! You take this grass that you were busy discovering just now. So foolishly trusting of it to come

56

up in this arid climate."

Glad to ease off into the subject of climate, Christie agreed vigorously. "All these tracks, too. I can't imagine why anything wants to live here."

"Wants? Who said anything about 'want'? Do you want to?" he asked quizzically.

"No!"

"And yet, you're here and I'm here and so is that curious crew back at the camp, all about to take effect on each other for better or for—" Burnett shook his head, frowning. "This is the kind of talk I shouldn't be indulging in. Not with you."

"Well, I'm not *that* young and tender," Christie protested. "Why shouldn't you talk to me?"

"It's just that you're not a turtle." Again the smile came like a stroke of light across his face. "Those tracks you were just pondering over a minute ago were made by one of our aged citizens with a heavy gait, weak eyes, and a hard shell. He's the kind I can speak to safely; he's satisfied with his way of life. Or at least you have to assume he is. He's fulfilling his turtlehood."

Christie shook her head, baffled. "You talk so—crazy."

" 'Crazy' "—Burnett ate a section of the orange thoughtfully—"is a word I have no patience with. It's too convenient." He was about to go on when, from the near distance, came a clangorous racket; it sounded as if someone were beating on a tin bucket. The man up on the bank uncurled and stretched.

"That unlovely sound summons me to go and earn

57

my keep," he explained. "Some poor mechanical invention is waiting to be personality-adjusted." He got to his feet and laughed shortly. "That look of yours—I read it. But you're wrong. I don't talk 'crazy,' little lady. You just listen that way."

7

And if somebody doesn't take effect on somebody, I'll go cr— Christie ducked the word, mentally, leaving the sentence all full of raw edges inside her.

How anybody could sit so still and be so lost to the world! She shot a glance at Joel, not two feet away on the other end of the bench in front of the station. Except for a word of greeting when he'd sat down, he hadn't so much as flickered a look in her direction. Right now he seemed engrossed in counting his shoelaces—pretty old shoelaces, spliced and knotted in several places. The shoes themselves were hard, heavy, workman's boots. Most men would have looked all feet in them, but Joel, with his long muscular shanks, wore them comfortably.

Christie had to admit, somewhat unwillingly, that his presence near her was once again sending that charge of excitement. Or was it aggravation? Doesn't real electricity have to work two ways? There he sat, as if he were a hundred miles from the nearest girl. Only sticking around, presumably, because Mabel hadn't come back with the mail yet.

She usually went right after lunch to pick it up at the Junction, a bigger crossroads with a post office, some miles away. Today she was late. As Christie looked out along the highway for the twentieth time, she was thinking she ought to be getting a letter from Rudy pretty soon. She'd written him some good letters herself—breezy, warm, careful not to overdo the loneliness bit, just enough to make him know she missed him. Three letters in two weeks. And the dog hadn't even sent her a postcard! Not that she was under any illusions about his pining away. Rudy never was a loner, and there were plenty of cute girls always available to a character with a Thunderbird. But you would think he'd still find a little heart left over for somebody who had once got him off the ground.

Men—! Christie returned to consideration of the one on the far end of the bench. Who'd be writing to him? she wondered. Some pert little strawberry picker —sunbonnet, rosy cheeks, pretty and curvish? That might account for this aloofness of his.

Impulsively she cast a remark into all that moody revery. "Don't you sometimes feel as if all your friends

60

are interplanetary? I mean, either they're out of this world or we are."

Joel glanced over, his face quickening with some response, although she had the notion he hadn't taken in what she'd said. Just seemed to be pleased that she'd spoken.

"I've been sitting here thinking," she went on, "about all the poor kids back there in high school, rushing around, stuffing all that sawdust into their heads. I guess I shouldn't blame them if they don't write. They probably hate me for escaping."

He seemed surprised. "You mean you haven't finished high school? I thought you'd probably already graduated."

"Not me," she assured him. Then, cautiously, she added, "How about you?"

"I only had three years." He said it as if it were over and done.

"Well, I never was a bookworm myself," she rattled along comfortably. "In fact, I've always had a terrific yen to just go out and pick oranges or something."

Joel seemed on the verge of being amused. "Pretty dirty work," he commented. "Come a good Santa Ana wind or two, with a lot of sand blowing, the grit settles out onto the orange trees. You go to pick the fruit, you get gray with it—it gets all over you, your hair, your eyes, in your teeth. Maybe you ought to try it, though— you might develop a taste for sawdust."

The sudden twist caught Christie so short it took her

61

a minute to realize just how he had turned her own words on her. She blinked at him, speechless, but Joel was looking off up the highway. The tow truck had come in sight.

Mabel always drove with both hands and a glassy look. She came off the road like a train jumping the track, tore past the old salt cedar, clipping a couple of fronds, and hauled up just short of the station in a kick of sand. As she got out, Wayne stopped grooming a car long enough to ask whether there was any mail.

"Yeah," she told him glumly. "Forms to fill out, to renew all the ever-lovin' licenses. Nothing for you, Joey. Sorry." Going on into the store, she dumped a handful of envelopes on the counter, picking through them. To Christie, who had followed her in, she handed three letters. "Your boy friends sure use strong perfume," she said cutely.

"They do that to confuse nosy people who snoop around my mail," retorted Christie, but her heart wasn't in it. The letters were all from girls. It was very discouraging.

When she went back out, Joel had sat down on the bench again; he didn't look sociable. So there must be some sort of feminine competition to explain this monumental no-take he was doing on her.

Reluctantly, she headed back home. Lately the parents were getting raspy enough to take off skin. It was turning out about as she had feared—Dad spent the days fussing around the trailer, and Mom was concentrating

62

on her poor violets so hard they were dying.

As she walked up the court, Christie noticed that Pete Moreno was out working on his car again—the hood was up. He and Joel had been spending hours hovering over the shook-up old engine as though it were a sick friend. Now it was McKinney with him.

And then she realized that there was something more going on than a discussion of nuts and bolts. Their postures were tense, and McKinney's voice twanged with rage.

"—I say you took it!"

Pete was shaking his head. "I take nothing, honest. I am no thief."

"You're a germ," snapped Mac furiously. "It'd be a public-health service if Slater'd run you out of here. Sneaking around, lifting stuff."

Instinctively, without having to think, Christie faded back and ran for the front of the station. Joel looked up as she burst around the corner.

"Pete's having trouble"—she pointed incoherently— "McKinney is—"

Joel came off the bench as if he'd been triggered. As he thrust past her, anger brought a blaze to his eyes that transformed his quiet face.

Christie, following at a safe distance, heard him call to Pete as he came up. She knew enough Spanish to understand what he said.

"Your fight is my fight."

"No, no." The Mexican put out a brown hand to restrain him. "We don't want no trouble. I didn't steal nothing, no need to fight."

McKinney snorted. "You better run along home, wipe your nose, sonny. This is between me and the wetback."

Christie felt the hair crawl on her neck, the way she used to feel when some smart-aleck policeman began to make wisecracks at the kids. Except that McKinney was no cop and Joel was no kid. His hands were clenched, but he held in.

In a level tone that vibrated with the effort of control, he said, "I don't want to fight you. Why don't you go on home now?"

"I came here to get my flashlight back and I'm gonna get it." McKinney's jaw jutted forward. "You Okies been picking things so long, you think you can pick up another guy's property like it was carrots. You're scavengers."

Christie saw Joel slip into gear. He was in motion—when another voice checked him.

"Hold it!" yelled Slater, coming up at a trot. "Anybody starts trouble gets kicked out." Getting between them, he demanded irritably, "Now what in blazes is going on? I don't want the Highway Patrol strutting around here. We can settle this. What's your beef, Mac?"

McKinney said impatiently, "I had a brand-new flashlight. I was working under my trailer this morning. So I guess I left it out front of my trailer while I go in for a little lunch. Now it's been swiped. I'm fed up—"

64

"Did you see who took it?" Slater cut in.

"Oh, Lord!" shouted McKinney. "If I saw him do it I'd have stopped him. For crying out loud!"

Wayne turned to Pete. "Did you take the flashlight?"

The little man shook his head anxiously, his brown face gleaming with perspiration like polished mahogany under the sun. Carefully he said, "I never stole nothing in my life."

Slater frowned. "You've got no case, Mac. Why start all this?"

"I started it? *I started it?* Listen," McKinney gargled, "it is not something for the Supreme Court to figure out how my—" He broke off and his look narrowed. "There's just one outside chance it could've been somebody else. Anybody seen the tramp lately?"

"The tramp is on the scene." From the far side of Pete's car Burnett got to his feet, brushing the loose grime from his coveralls. "Excuse me for not joining you sooner, but I was lying there contemplating the differential. Not of the car," he added thoughtfully. "The differential that separates the men from the jackasses."

McKinney went red as raw meat. "Who you calling a jackass?"

Burnett smiled. "Does the saddle pinch?"

"How'd you like to get your teeth shoved down your throat?"

Leaning on the fender, wiping off the wrench he'd been using, Burnett said, "I agree with Pedro. Physical violence is no solution. I myself prefer theory. You take Mr. McKinney's first theory, that Pete stole his flashlight, and his second theory—that I took it. Interesting, but not practical, since Pete and I have been working on this crate since ten o'clock this morning. That makes a new theory necessary. And I think I have it for you." Again he smiled at McKinney, but this time Christie saw that it put no light into his face; it was more the smile of an executioner who enjoys swinging the ax.

"The logical answer," he went on, "is that Pete and I were in collusion. We must have planned this caper jointly and are alibying each other. Tonight, of course, we'll divide the loot: he'll take one battery and I'll take the other—I assume it was only a two-cell?"

"Kit." The quiet word startled Christie. She whirled to find that her father had come up behind her. He motioned toward their trailer and she knew better than to argue. Leaving the gentle voice of Burnett, boring in like a sharp bit, and McKinney beginning to give off sparks, she tagged along unhappily, resentful at having to miss the end of the scene.

And yet, before they had even reached their own doorstep, the circle back there had broken up, McKinney striding off to his own lot and Slater loping for the front of the station where a car had just pulled in.

"Are you coming?" Her father prompted her in a tone which meant that the next scheduled event would be a lecture.

The card table was definitely too small to eat dinner on that evening. The three of them sat there, knee to knee and no appetite. Christie didn't really think it had been such an awful thing, to stand and watch a play of emotions, to escape, momentarily, the crush of boredom.

Not that Dad had been ferocious. Just laid down the law, that was all. Stay close to home. Don't dawdle around the court. Don't mix into any arguments or visit with the other "elements" of the community. Of course it was perfectly okay for Dad to hobnob with McKinney. He wasn't an "element" presumably. Christie wondered bitterly why these discrepancies can't be pointed out to parents. She usually let Dad's editorials trickle off, but this was slightly different. She couldn't just ignore him and do as she pleased because he was around all the time, watching.

Tentatively she asked, "But don't you think Pedro is all right? He was nice to us that first day."

"Christin, I do not want you to argue with me." Dad spoke firmly. "We came out here for relaxation. My— my stomach is getting upset. The doctor said I might have an ulcer any day now. So let's let the subject drop."

Meanly Christie said, "All right, but sometimes I feel like if I can't ask questions or talk or go anywhere or speak to anybody, *I'll go mad!*" Her voice came high and thin—not entirely by intention. She saw Mom and Dad exchange anxious looks.

"Well, dear, naturally you can ask questions, and we'd be so glad if you would talk to us. Just tell us anything!" Mom urged hastily. "Tomorrow maybe you and I can go for a nice walk out in the desert. I can't think of a better place to just talk and talk."

Christie put down her fork. "Would you mind if I don't finish my dinner?"

"Now, hon!" Dad frowned miserably. "You need your food. You ought to gain some weight."

"I'm not hungry."

"Kit— You do understand why I've asked you to disassociate yourself from these people, don't you?"

She shook her head.

"Well"—he squirmed—"in the first place, they're transients. They can't have much sense of responsibility, to wander aimlessly, living a hand-to-mouth existence. They come from different backgrounds—"

"Do you think Pete Moreno would steal?" she asked relentlessly.

"That's not the point. I admit that he seems like a decent sort. It's more likely that the road bum is light-fingered."

"Why?" she demanded naïvely.

"Now don't ask nonsense questions. You certainly are aware of the type of man who roves the highways of the country."

"Well, I know, but Burnett doesn't talk like that type."

"His tongue is a bit too quick," her father retorted dryly. "It's one of the most suspect features about him. I wouldn't be surprised if he is in hiding from the bunko squad."

"But to take a flashlight would be so *silly*."

68

"I grant you it's a petty matter. What is not so minor" —he glanced from one to the other of them—"is that two nights ago my wrist watch was stolen from the glove compartment of the car."

Mom gasped. "Your good one?"

"No, it wasn't the good one. But a thirty-dollar watch is a thirty-dollar loss. I didn't see any point of making an issue of it. I shouldn't have left the car window down. But it brought home to me sharply the fact that we're surrounded by a polyglot array of itinerants who are obviously wretchedly poor. The temptation was just too much for somebody."

"Maybe we ought to move on," Mom suggested, tizzyish.

"I've thought of it, but I'd rather not. From many aspects, this is a healthful, convenient place to winter." Dad seemed to try not to shudder. "As long as we keep on the lookout, I'm sure we can cope with slight dishonesty. Even with Mr. Burnett's subversive undertones."

"Why do you say 'subversive'?" Christie asked, perplexed. "He hasn't plugged for socialized medicine or anything. Just because Wayne called him a radical—"

"My dear, any man of his obvious intellect who chooses to be a drifter either has something to hide, something illegal to sell, or"— Dad paused ominously— "a dangerous philosophy."

"Maybe he just likes to wander. Maybe he doesn't want to settle down and be a union man." The least bit of scorn crept into her tone and Dad stepped on it.

"Kit, I have let you go on with your questioning because I want you to see things clearly. You apparently find something glamorous about Mr. Burnett, and your warm heart tends to make you sympathetic with the less fortunate members of our camp. There is nothing particularly colorful about Mr. McKinney, and I believe I detect some deprecation of him on your part. So let me explain the fault of your reasoning. McKinney has his crudities, I grant you, but he's a working man. He has a reasonable education and a fairly good experience in his own line. He doesn't drink, he carries life insurance, he keeps up with what is going on in the world. In his own way he fits a part that is necessary in our economy, the role of labor. While not a man I would necessarily consort with by choice, let's say he's a man I would hire. When you romanticize the unstable or picaresque characters of a group, you show immaturity. I hope you'll rise above it one of these days. Once you learn to analyze certain values, you'll be a long way toward growing up."

In the early gray twilight of dawn, lying limp and still half asleep, Christie felt another kind of awakening, an awareness stretching off in new directions. Beyond the walls of the lonesome little cubbyhole of a room were people. But no longer set up in neat columns under headings: parents, teachers, kids. . . . And Dad's categories wouldn't work for her, either. This was a crowd of

70

people who said strange, unreasonable things, or else their reasoning was complicated and hidden—people with fierce emotions burning inside, quirks of temper that she couldn't understand. Snatches of talk kept playing back. . . .

". . . the differential . . ."

". . . your fight is my fight . . ."

". . . subversive overtones . . ."

Christie's rambling thoughts snagged on that all over again. How could Burnett be proven subversive—radical? And yet he himself had warned her that he was dangerous. In some secret way.

As for being drifters, weren't they all? The Fords, too, at least right now.

And McKinney. A good joe, until he began to talk mean. Did being in the union make that okay? Then a different yardstick would have to be set up, because remembering the sneer on his face still put her back up like ten cats. Immaturity? The word goaded her sharply.

Christie closed her eyes and saw a vivid mental image of the redheaded man standing above her on the bank—that lean face with its smile, challenging her. *Little lady, you only listen crazy.*

Restless and confused, Christie sat up wide-eyed. Shivering in the chill of morning, she looked toward the window where yellow daylight was spreading a pale wash over the eastern sky.

So—she vowed thoughtfully—I will listen cool.

71

PART
II

Joel

In the boundless blazing silence of the land, time seemed to hang still. Not just the hours but the days themselves, as though the ticking of all the clocks in the world had stopped. Here there was no sense of the future lurking somewhere just ahead, out of sight, like a pit.

Not that Christie had come to like this desolation, but she did find herself moving at an easier rhythm. As she sorted out some washing she caught herself humming slow songs, jailhouse blues. She even had to admit that the work didn't seem so hateful as it had back home, where she had begrudged every minute of time at the laundromat. Waiting for the impassive machine to cycle, she had wanted to kick it into hurrying. Now as she put the colored clothes in one pile, the white laundry in another, there was no sense of rush.

From the front room she could hear her parents' voices. Mom's chirping seemed a little subdued these days; Dad was getting quieter, too, but it was a grim quiet.

He'd gone on a new tangent lately. Day after day he would sit at the card table going over the old account records of a furniture business that was no longer his—books that had been audited and closed, officially, when he'd sold the shop. All Dad would say, in explanation, was that he was "analyzing" them.

This was so peculiar it was even worrying Mom. Although she tried not to show it, surreptitiously she kept trying to pry him away from this gloomy work. As Christie finished bundling up the laundry, she heard her mother say something, Dad snapping back.

"Stella, I do not want to take a walk!"

It had been like this ever since that awful Thanksgiving week end. Something about going through the motions of the holiday had been grisly. Turkey had never tasted drier. It seemed to bring home to all of them the pointlessness of celebrating some ancient tradition which certainly had nothing to do with the Ford family. Christie was almost afraid to think what Christmas would be like.

Her mother was evidently worrying about it, too. As Christie came into the front room Mom was saying,

76

"Sam, you know we really ought to start making out our Christmas-card list."

"I'm not going to send any this year," he answered shortly.

"But, pet—!"

"What sort of rank hypocrisy would it be, to beam out cheerful little messages to all our friends? You do it if you like, Stella."

Christie eased on out the door, leaving them in their miserable tableau—Dad glaring at his ledger, Mom hovering over her last remaining violet.

The desert was too rough for violets. Right now as Christie stepped out into the brightness she felt an impulse to wilt, too, although she'd found it wasn't really so violent as it looked. The cloudless sky was like a sheet of hot brass, the distant mountains shimmered through the sun waves, and yet the air was dry; it was pleasant in the shade.

The laundry room was a particularly cool spot—just an adobe shed hitched onto the back of the garage, with two sets of concrete tubs and one cranky old washing machine that operated on a pay-as-you-go basis. But there was something restful about it—the slosh of suds and the steady beat of the power plant next door, the regular pumping of the well.

In this particular place Christie could even enjoy being alone. She felt almost resentful when she heard someone else coming—probably Mrs. McKinney, a plump gabby woman who loved to trot over and gossip with anyone doing washing. Intently Christie kept her back turned to the door and went on poking the sheets down into the hot water with the end of a broomstick. But the steps came on, hesitated at the threshold, and when no one spoke, she finally had to turn. Looking over her shoulder, she saw Joel standing there uncertainly.

He was carrying a small bundle of Levis and shirts, a bar of soap, and a scrubbing brush. He must have seen lingering traces of irritation in her face, because he asked, "Will I be in your way?"

Rapidly reorganizing, Christie smiled warmly. "Not at all! Come on in. We can take turns on the machine. As soon as these sheets are finished, you can—"

"Thanks. I never use it, just a tub." Turning on the hot water, he dumped the whole wad of clothes in carelessly, picked out a pair of Levis, plastered them against the side of the tub, and began to scour them with the brush. It seemed fairly primitive to Christie, but Joel went about it as though it were old habit.

As he bent over the work, he remarked, "It's been quite a while since I saw you around. I thought maybe you were under the weather."

On the brink of a bright evasion, Christie broke off and reconsidered. It occurred to her that it couldn't be pure coincidence that Joel had turned up here just five minutes after she had marched down the court with a pillowcase full of laundry. Encouraged by the discovery, she decided to speak on a more confidential note.

"My father was pretty burned at me for standing in on that scene McKinney made last week. He said it wasn't ladylike to hang around where men are arguing."

"Wasn't too safe," Joel agreed. "That could have got rough."

"I was prepared to take cover." Then growing more earnest she added, "It was good to see somebody stand up for something for once! I wished you could have gone on and poked McKinney in the snoot. People are getting meaner every day. If I were a man, I'd bust anybody that talked sarcastic, or bullied nice people like Mr. Moreno."

Joel gave her a look that was definitely more friendly than any he'd handed out before. "I told Pete it was you who came and called me that day. He felt good about it. Not many folks have been kind to the Morenos. I'm sorry it got you in Dutch."

"Oh, I'm used to that," she assured him. "I'm always being lectured on how I'm not a little lady. I guess I was born with a chip on my shoulder. I hate all big-shot types, the stupid wisecracks and the way they sneer—" Somehow the talk had gotten more serious than she'd intended. Watch out, Kit, she warned herself, play it light!

And yet Joel was listening thoughtfully. "I know what you mean. There are a lot of people who gall me. But do you fight them? I mean does it improve things to sock somebody?" He was really asking her for an answer.

"Well, it would certainly make me feel better!" she burst out honestly.

"I know, that's why I used to get into so many fights —I mean with other kids, back when I was in school. You have to learn there; the part of New York where I lived is no place for a sissy to walk the street after dark."

"You lived in New York City!"

He glanced over at her with a quirk to his lips that aged him by years. "Did you think I was a native-born field hand?"

"N-no, but I didn't—"

"I grew up on the West Side, in Manhattan. You've got to learn to size people. Sometimes you better be ready to jump them before they jump you, especially if they're carrying some sort of advantage. That's why—" He broke off and wrung out the pair of Levis hard enough to sprain the seams. Finally he said, "I guess you ought to know about it."

Sensing that he was teetering on the brink of not telling her what she ought to know about, Christie kept still.

"A few weeks back," he went on slowly, "I really got in a fight. It was when we were over in Texas. I went into a hamburger shop with some other pickers—Mexicans. There was a dirty-necked customer there, began to make remarks about the others, about me being with them. I figured that was my business, but this seedy character wouldn't let us alone. You'd think he was part of the royal family and we were trash. The others had

80

to keep quiet—a Mexican doesn't dare speak up. But I talked back. The loud-mouth was some bigger than me and he had a knife—I saw the line of it under his shirt. So as he was getting ready to go into action, I closed in first. It was quite a ruckus," he finished dryly. "We both landed in jail."

"You mean the dirty cops wouldn't even let you defend yourself?"

"They're supposed to keep the peace." He shrugged. "If anybody was doing the defending, I guess it was the other fellow. I was pretty mad."

She waited for him to go on, but he didn't. Scrubbing away at a faded work shirt, he appeared to be lost in thoughts that blanked out the world around him. She saw a look almost like a spasm of pain cross his face.

"What happened then?" she ventured at last.

With a start he roused. "Oh. Nothing. I mean, I sat there in the tank all night and wondered what had been proved. Except that the other guy had a sore jaw. Didn't make the inside of his head any decenter. He'll still do the same thing over and over. How does anybody do anything to improve anything?" With a trace of anger he tossed the brush down and wrung out the shirt.

"Was the judge unkind?"

"No, he was okay. Let us both off for a fine. Pete paid mine; I didn't have the cash at the time."

"You must be very good friends."

"Ever since then he and his wife have been like a family to me. I don't know why." Joel looked at her wonderingly. "But there's one thing I do know: Pete gets along without fighting."

But Pete isn't going anywhere—the answer crossed her mind, though she didn't speak it. Pete knows he can't expect much, not the way things are set up, so he isn't bucking it. He'll never be anything but a picker. But you . . .?

"Joel, I hope," she said tentatively, "that you don't think I—or I mean a girl—would ever feel it was something down-grading to have spent a night in the deep-freeze. Not for a reasonable reason like that!"

He smiled almost naturally. "Some would. I wasn't sure about you—you're not the kind of person I've ever met out here."

"You've been here a long time?"

"Not right here. But there are a hundred other camps like this all over the southwest, little gravel patches where people go to wait out the next harvest. Or like those old men, they wait to die."

The grimness of that thought and the way he said it reminded Christie that the conversation was getting ten feet deep again. Struggling to get back on the surface, she said, "Well, we've got a long way to go before we ossify, I hope. How old are you, Joel?"

"Nineteen."

"You seem older."

"Maybe that's because I've been kicking around the fields for three years."

But why? It lay there in the silence, as plain as if it

82

had been shouted out loud, and yet Christie couldn't bring herself to say the word.

"Of course it's a healthy life," she chattered on nervously, "if you don't get flattened by the boredom. All this sunshine may be full of vitamins, but don't you yen for the known world, once in a while—a good rocking jukebox or even a tarnished television bit?"

He was rolling his wash all up together, frowning as if she had puzzled him.

"I mean, when they say 'from nowhere' they're talking about here," she bubbled even more urgently as she saw him distinctly getting ready to go. "I heard there was some kind of town over east a way. Even if it's got a population of thirteen, it would look good to me right now."

For a city-bred boy, even three years removed, Joel certainly wasn't operating on her wave length.

"I mean," she tried to put it in basic English, "I am homesick for a good time, even a small one."

"You don't have to translate," he said, not too kindly. "I just don't feel for all that, myself. Seems like a long way back . . ." He didn't finish that one. Looking across at her curiously, he said, "You told me your name is Kit. Does that stand for Katherine?"

She shook her head. "Christin. The folks used to call me Christie until I picked up the new look in high school."

"Oh." He nodded, as if she'd just explained something. Then, ducking his head in a quaint little gesture

83

of politeness, he said, "I've got to go on back now. See you again."

Abruptly the washing machine cut off and left the room silent. As Christie stood staring after the lanky figure crossing the court, she felt as disconnected as the mechanical gadget beside her. Unhappily she began to search her coin purse for another quarter.

"Crazy," she said aloud. "Absolutely crazy."

"There's that easy word again."

She jerked up to see Burnett standing the narrow opening that connected the laundry room with the garage. Munching his orange, he regarded her critically. It was maddening to have him just materialize that way. With the shock of red hair and probing, tawny eyes, it was like having the Devil pop up out of a stage door in *Faust*.

"I think you've short-changed that young man," he added. "Joel is worth a good half-dozen words at least."

"Where did you— What were you doing there?"

"Eavesdropping. I often do. It can be very enlightening."

Angrily she shoved the coin in the machine and it started to splash again. "It's not gentlemanly to listen to other people's conversations."

"I agree. But sometimes it's the only way you can find things out, and I'd rather be informed than formal. In this case," Burnett added, "I felt it particularly justified. After peregrinating as long and far as I have, I'm not usually baffled by people, so when I cross the path of

84

someone complex, I consider it a matter of scientific research to try to figure them."

"Why should I baffle you?" she demanded.

"You don't, little lady. The young man is the case in point."

His answer disarmed Christie to the extent that her aggravation thinned out and she faced him soberly. "Do you think so, too? That Joel's complex, I mean."

"So much so that it disturbs me. He's no baby, and he's not a clod. In fact, his reaction to you today showed remarkable perception. To question your name . . ."

"That was the cra— I mean, the complexest thing of all. To ask about that, right when—"

As she hesitated, Burnett smiled. "Right when you were making your pitch for a date."

It wasn't quite comfortable to be so understood. "Well, I was just—making talk—"

"Exactly. And his question wasn't so irrelevant right then as you suppose. If you hadn't been concentrating so hard on your technique, you'd have seen what he was getting at."

Christie stared at him, confused.

Burnett led her a step further. "If Joel insisted on being called 'Shorty,' wouldn't you wonder what he was trying to prove?" He tossed a handful of orange peel into the wastebasket. "I've got to get back to work. Besides, at this point you ought to take a turn at the wheel. Your intuition is a bit rusty—some practice will do it good. Without intuition a woman is a shell."

"Wait. What did you mean?" She followed over to the entrance way. "You're always getting me confused and then walking off."

He had already gone back to lean over the engine of the car he was servicing. Without looking up he said, "The only advice I could offer would be for you to get acquainted with Señora Moreno. But then you can't do that, can you? It would be against orders." Wresting something from the innards of the car, he held it up to look at it—a small piece of hose, frayed and ruptured. Almost to himself he remarked, "Ruined. Too much pressure? Or faulty specifications?"

9

Christie stopped brushing her hair long enough to stare at herself suspiciously in the mirror. It was small, like everything else in the trailer—just big enough to frame her face, tanned and un-made-up and grave right now. The light hair floated loose about it, electric from the brushing, pale as natural silk from the bleach of the sunlight. The curl, once so carefully coaxed, had been loosening out of it, leaving a straight fall that was more flattering than she would have believed.

Kit? she questioned her image critically. Kit was a girl with a shiny finish—a chrome job. Kit had a mouth carefully designed out of lipstick, to make laughter with. Now, without the art work, her expression had somehow grown warmer. The straight line of her lips, which she'd always thought too firm to be charming, suddenly seemed right with the rest of her.

Glancing down at the slim body in blue jeans and starched blue-checkered shirt, Christie thought that this was a girl Rudy wouldn't look at twice. And yet she had to admit that it was a relief, just to be natural for a while. Apparently it wasn't entirely unattractive or Joel wouldn't have shown that slow-growing appreciation when they had talked together in the laundry room. He'd liked her best when she was being serious.

So, Mr. Burnett, my intuition isn't as squeaky as you think!

Christie went on out of the bedroom; in the kitchen she found her mother, sitting on a stool, sipping a cup of coffee. Stella smiled at her, but she seemed strangely quiet. Ever since Dad had left for Los Angeles early this morning some of the high pressure had gone out of the house.

It had been no small project to get him to go. Christie had watched in amazement as Mom had executed a series of strategic maneuvers. First she'd developed a need for a bunch of necessary household items that just couldn't be purchased anywhere but the city. Then she'd made out a list of Christmas presents, equally unheard of here in the desert. Finally she'd discovered a crack in her bridgework that just had to be fixed by her own dentist. For sheer inventiveness, that one really tied all records, Christie had to admit.

So, in the end, Dad had grumpily packed a suitcase

and driven off westward where he would undoubtedly have a fine week end looking up his old cronies and roaming the Christmas-decked stores. If the trip didn't pep him up, they might as well resign themselves to a miserable holiday. But the real point was that Christie had discovered Mom employing feminine tricks such as she never had before, and doing it well. The secret knowledge made her feel closer to her mother for some reason.

It even encouraged her to wonder if she could maybe talk frankly about things. Helping herself to a cup of coffee—the cocoa routine couldn't very well be pretended with Dad gone—she sat down on the other counter stool.

"I don't think the desert is doing Dad as much good as the doctor thought," she remarked innocently.

Stella studied the hot drink without answering at once, as if for a minute she were tempted to spill the truth about the situation. Then the impulse must have passed.

With a transparent effort at cheeriness she said, "Oh, he's doing marvelously, I think. I'm sure he's relaxing."

"Mom!" Christie protested softly. "Don't kid me."

And so, as if she were suddenly tired of her own forced gaiety, Stella fell silent. At last she said, troubled, "Your father is concerned about the future. It's a bitter experience for a man his age to see a business fail."

"You think that's why he keeps adding up the score? To find out where he went wrong?"

89

Her mother nodded. "Something like that. Trying to figure out how he could go at it differently next time, if 'next time' comes."

"But why is he bearing down so hard? Out here you don't feel time rushing at you; it's the one fair feature of the place."

Stella regarded her fondly. "I can remember—not so long ago, either—when I felt the same way. I didn't see why I should bother figuring out what comes next. Problems were for somebody else to worry about. Bills got paid out of a checkbook. And I wasn't ever going to get old." She laughed at her own fancy. "You always think you're going to raise your children differently—make them marvelously realistic and self-reliant. But when the time comes, you just hope they stay young as long as possible. Kitty, I'm glad you aren't troubling yourself about the future. I shouldn't even talk about it. For a while life should be all fun."

Kindly as it was meant, the whole idea of being considered juvenile and lightheaded made Christie smart.

"Oh, sure," she answered edgily, "this place is a barrel of kicks. Especially since I can't associate with any of the 'elements.'"

"Now, dear, you know your father is only thinking of your welfare."

"It would probably do my welfare more good if I was allowed to make up my own mind about people," Christie asserted recklessly. "How will I ever develop all that judgment he wants me to have if he doesn't let me meet people and learn for myself? I'm getting *frustrated!*" It was kind of mean and she knew it, but it worked. Mom began to look worried.

"Could you tell me what it is that's bothering you, dear? Maybe I could help."

"I don't see why you should blackball somebody just because somebody else calls him a 'germ.' If it's sanitary to be like Mrs. McKinney and gossip all day about how Mabel flirts with the truck drivers then I'd just as soon take a chance on the Morenos. They look more decent to me, and they're certainly a lot quieter. How does Dad *know* they're an 'element'?"

Stella grew still again, apparently once more on the verge of some confession. "I don't—I really don't think your father meant—" Then irrelevantly she said, "I heard their baby was sick. A cold or something?"

"Sore throat." Christie unlimbered the intuition. "Poor little thing can't shake it off. Probably doesn't get enough to eat. Nobody ever goes over to visit them. I'll bet Mrs. Moreno thinks everybody here is against her."

Mom's eyes were soft as a pansy.

"Listen"—Christie pushed her advantage eagerly— "why couldn't I drop over and just—you know—take something to the baby? Would that be so terrible?"

Stella looked up at her, all unfocused and human. "I think," she said, "some honey would be nice."

But when, a half-hour later, Christie stood in front of the Morenos' doorstep with a jar of honey in her hand, she wasn't exactly sure just why she had wanted to come.

Part compassion, of course, but also it was partly due to Burnett's cryptic suggestion.

The few times Christie had seen Pete's wife, she had been only a dark, lonely figure dressed in long skirts, her head covered with a black shawl. She seldom stayed outside more than a minute or two at a time. From a distance she had appeared somber. Now as she opened the door Christie saw that she was as full of color as a glowing ember. She was quite tall, and the fullness of her body was in rich proportion. Although she didn't smile, the serenity of the liquid dark eyes was warm.

"Señora"—Christie summoned all the poise she could manage—"I heard that your little girl has a cold. I thought she might like some honey." The rehearsed speech faltered toward the end.

The woman in the doorway studied her an instant silently. Under the challenge of that look Christie thought any insincerity would start giving off smoke. Then the Señora opened the door and took the gift.

"It is nice. Thank you. You will come in?"

Stepping inside, Christie was surprised to find Joel there. He got to his feet with that courtesy that was practically Victorian. So did Pete. There was about the whole room an old-time graciousness that was hard to define, inasmuch as the trailer was very poorly furnished—a threadbare rug, a few pieces of scarred furniture. Everything was ruthlessly clean, but then Christie had expected that. She'd been in Mexican homes before, visiting some of her school friends in Los Angeles, and it had seemed as though the housewives never stopped scrubbing. Here, though, she felt something that went deeper than surface cleanliness. She noticed in the far corner of the room a votive candle flickering before a statuette of the Madonna.

Pete was ushering her forward now to their best seat —an old overstuffed armchair near the front window. The Señora had gone to the sink to open the jar of honey while Joel pursued the baby, who had crawled away under one of the chairs. Gently he picked the child up, handling her with an easy grace that seemed to come naturally to him, and brought her back to set her on the pile of comforters in the center of the floor. The Señora put a spoonful of honey in a little twist of clean cloth and gave it to the little girl, who sucked it soberly, staring at Christie with a look that seemed too large and bright for the thin, elfish little face.

As they sat around awkwardly, Pete set his hands on his knees, smiling. "This is one fine day, yes."

"It certainly is!" Christie smiled back.

Joel had picked up a piece of wood he'd been whittling and was working at it intently again.

The Señora glanced around. "You would like some coffee maybe?"

But it was the baby who pulled the string that tumbled the barriers. With sudden intentness she crawled across and laid hold of Christie's chair, hauling herself up to stand teetering, staring in solemn fascination. In a stroke of perception Christie realized what the attraction was.

Scooping the dark little bundle into her lap, she let the small hands reach out and grab the shimmering locks around her face.

"See? She likes my hair!" Christie laughed.

The Morenos smiled. And Joel looked at her as if he were discovering some private miracle of his own.

As they ate a sparse lunch around a homemade table, the one thing that struck Christie was that they could all talk together as if they were of the same age and spirit. The conversation was as warm and satisfying as the re-fried beans.

"Oh, she's a good cook, my wife," Pete said proudly.

The Señora smiled. "Anything tastes good to a hungry man. The real gift is like what Joel has, the way he can use the knife. Show the doll you make for the baby."

The boy tried to protest, but they wouldn't stop coaxing until he brought out his carving—a doll's head; the laughing little Mexican face was whittled out of a beautiful dark wood.

"That's ironwood," he explained. "It grows down along these draws. Good to carve."

"This is lovely, Joel!" Christie held it a minute, truly surprised at the skill of the work. "Where did you learn to do this?"

"Oh, Joel's been to school," Pete told her. "He even been to high school some."

"You didn't learn something like this in school." Christie handed back the carving.

Joel seemed to withdraw and fold into himself right

94

before her eyes. "No," he said, "I didn't." And if ever a subject was closed, that was.

"Listen, Joel," Pete got suddenly serious, "did you learn about the income taxes in that school? Pretty soon I reckon I got to pay."

The boy looked puzzled. "You made over eighteen hundred dollars this year?"

"Santa Maria, no!" Pete shouted.

"Then you don't have to pay any income tax. They allow you that much for three people to live."

The Mexican looked dubious. "I don't know. I think if you got some left you have to pay, what they say, extra-profits tax. I don't want no trouble with the government, only I wished I could tell them how I need a clutch. Burnett says the old car can't pull this box no more."

"Listen"—Joel looked up, frowning. "Let me fool with that clutch a while longer. I don't trust Burnett. He's probably trying to make a buck off you."

"Why you say that?" Pete asked innocently. "He done a lot of work already and he never took pay."

"He's got an angle," Joel insisted doggedly. "He must. Everybody's got some kind of angle."

The Señora looked at Joel, her eyes full of affection and something akin to pity. "I don't think this with Burnett."

Christie had noticed that the men always listened when the woman put in a quiet word.

This time, unwillingly, Joel took issue with her. "But, Señora, why should he do anybody any favors?" Then,

95

as if he read some unspoken answer in her faint smile, he flushed. "I mean, he doesn't seem like a kind sort of person. He's too smart—he's got too many answers."

"This can be hard, to have many answers," the Señora said patiently. "Why you do not like him, Joel? Has he hurt you?"

"No. It's just the whole idea of him, drifting in for no reason, asking questions . . ."

Again the Señora smiled. "But if a man has all the answers, why must he ask the questions? No, Joel, I think this is a lonely man. He has no woman. When there is no one to stand with, a man drifts."

"Maybe that's why he doesn't have one," Christie suggested. "If a fellow likes to wander around free, I guess he'd rather not have a girl." She was watching Joel as she spoke.

"Or maybe," the boy said, "he's got no faith in anything. You couldn't ask a girl to go with you when you feel like everything's a bust."

"Joel. Don't you know?" The Señora reproached him mildly. "This is when a man needs a wife most."

The low-spoken words kept stirring in Christie's mind as she lay awake late that night. They implied a terrible responsibility—beyond anything she'd yet realized in her casual thoughts about marriage. It had always seemed to her a kind of protection, to marry some man who would provide, make the decisions, lend her the strength of his masculine stability. It hadn't occurred

96

to her that a woman might have to be the stronger of the two sometimes.

She thought of her mother; she'd always taken it for granted that Mom was the silly type who would go off in all directions except for Dad. She was positive that Dad thought so. And yet this morning the camera had focused from a different angle. It even seemed possible that if Mom didn't talk so much, somebody might pay attention to her, too. Or was it the other way around, and maybe she talked on and on because nobody did listen?

Restlessly Christie kicked off the covers and got up. It was a warm night for the desert. Pulling the blinds up, she looked out across the vast, flat land steeped in moonlight, silver-plated and motionless. She was wishing she could remember just what she'd said to Joel, all those words so carelessly spoken. She tried to remember just which ones had touched off his inexplicable moods, what ones had established the few instants of communication. . . .

Her attention was distracted by a movement out in the breathless night. Someone was skirting the rear of the camp—a woman. She looked back over her shoulder once and the moonlight shone full on her face. It was Mabel. Moving stealthily, she went down the sleeping court and into the darkened house.

As chilled as though her path had just been crossed by a black cat, Christie went back to bed, to lie staring up into the darkness, thinking.

97

10

Sometime early in the small hours of the morning a drift of air stirred across the face of the desert, just a mild breeze that fingered the dry bushes, nudged the thorny branches of the scrub trees in the bottoms of the draws. It slid over the shallow wrinkles in the land where the green growth still lived precariously. The shoots were up an inch by now, putting out leaves that wore a soft coating of gray fur over the green, to protect them against the sun. They whispered faintly as the light wind touched them.

Christie wakened to the sound of the air streaming in her window, shivering the slats of the blinds. After the long hush, it was a welcome sound, even the small skeletal clashing of the arms of the dead bush under her window. Getting up, she dressed quickly; when she went into the front of the trailer she found her mother up early, too. Already finished with breakfast, she was deep in a list she was making out.

Glancing up at Christie anxiously, she said, "Christmas coming in the middle of the week means we won't have any really fresh carrots for carrot sticks."

So she was going ahead with plans for the usual feast. Christie dropped a light kiss on her mother's cheek and went over to the stove where eggs and bacon were laid out ready. As she ate, she could look across the court to where the breeze was beginning to snap the clothes that somebody had left out on the line behind the laundry. The salt cedar was tossing its willowy branches almost wildly.

"This is a nice, brisk day," she remarked, as she finished the dishes. "I think I'll go for a walk." Then abruptly she added, "But I'll go to the store for you first. What do you need?" She had just seen someone familiar head that way.

Joel's long-legged stride never seemed hurried, but it covered ground. By the time Christie got outside he had already disappeared around the front of the station. She followed, muttering to herself ". . . eggs, bread, coffee, catsup, eggs, bread . . ."

When she came into the store, Mabel had just put some things into a sack. Joel was paying her in small change.

Nodding to Christie, he said, "Morning."

"Hi." She smiled at them both.

Mabel looked worse than usual. Her hair evidently missed the pin curlers judging by the way it slumped around her face, and her eyes were sleepy and disgruntled. Bad night? Christie asked privately. Weren't there any watches in anybody's glove compartment? Lost all that sleep and no loot, maybe?

The more she had lain awake and thought about it last night, the more Christie felt reasonably sure that Mabel was not only capable of hooking valuables that didn't belong to her, but was really the most logical suspect. The way she grabbed every cent that came across the counter was pitiful. Now she punched the cash register irritably, as if disgusted with it for not being loaded with riches. The sale to Joel was only forty-two cents. He was turning to go.

"Hey," Christie smiled at him, "if you can hold up a minute I'll walk with you. I just need a few things."

Flushing slightly, he said, "I wish I could but—I've—I've got to get back right away." For the first time the fire-blue eyes faltered and seemed to avoid hers as he went on out of the store.

Mabel's face was completely readable—and nauseating. Her bitter contempt wasn't even in partial control this morning; it curled her lips.

"You little chasers really have to be hit over the head with a board before you see light," she said between her teeth.

In her hatred the girl was so ugly that Christie suddenly felt sorry for her. The old combative urge drained

100

away; it would have been sad to bandy catcalls with this poor witch.

"May I have a dozen eggs, please," she said patiently, "and—"

"Oh, yes, madam, you *may!*" Mabel didn't move. Her arms were rigid at her sides. "Other people mayn't, but you may. Boy, do you make me laugh, with your silly little baby-white hands. I'll bet you can't even wash dishes. I'll bet you never scrubbed a toilet in your life. Daddy gives you money and you come and buy eggs and toss off a smirk at the lower classes."

Christie didn't answer. Her very silence seemed to goad Mabel more than any retort could have.

"Why don't you ask Joey when he last had any eggs!" the girl was yelling. "He didn't buy anything but potatoes and salt pork for a month now. Ask him why he sits out on that bench! You think it's love letters he's waiting for? He's waiting to get word from the government where there's crops coming in. So you think you'd like to go out with him, like slumming, maybe? All this big-eye you're giving him—*I'll walk with you, Joey*— Well, you'll walk all right any time you go out with him, because he don't have enough in his jeans to buy a gallon of gas for joy riding. So what do you care? You torture a guy just for kicks!"

Christie turned and went out of the store. Dazed, she headed home, hardly aware of where she was going. Not that Mabel's venom had hurt her; it was what she'd said that had made the impact.

She was almost to the trailer when she was aware

101

that someone was coming along behind her; it was Joel, hurrying to catch up. As he confronted her, the wind gusted harder than before—it whipped the dark hair loose across his forehead. His face, too, had a driven look.

"I'm sorry," he said bluntly. "I didn't mean to be rude back there in the store."

"That's all right," she said. "I probably sounded too eager. I didn't mean to promote anything; it's just that I did enjoy that afternoon we spent with the Morenos the other day." She'd spoken simply, and she saw the sincere words take a grip on Joel that almost paralyzed him for a minute. A whole world of wishing showed in his eyes before he could hide it.

"So did I, Christie. Maybe too much. There are problems—I can't tell you, I can't talk about them. But I've made up my mind it isn't right to just see you enough so that I—we both—get—" He bogged down.

"Joel"—she made one more try as he seemed about to retreat—"it may be jumping to conclusions, but I'd like you to know that if it's money—if you think I need expensive entertainment or *any* entertainment to make me happy—that's no issue."

He shook his head like a horse under tight rein. "I know. Don't you think I know that? Christie, I'm no good for you. Don't make me try to spell it all out. I can't do it." Turning in a rush, he strode back down the court, leaving her deserted in the rising tide of wind.

Hardly thinking what she was doing, where she was going, Christie moved with it. It shoved her slowly

102

along. She saw the top sand being picked up and scattered ahead of her, the hard-swept little grasses bending flat, almost torn loose from their slender roothold. She felt as if she, too, were ripping away. The hand of the wind kept pressing against her back, urging her forward. She wanted to run with it, away from the tight little knot of people in The Oasis, all snarled up together with their boredom and their fears and their mysteries. . . .

In the comparative shelter of the big wash she walked along blindly. The vivid picture before her was of Joel. Her face burned with embarrassment as she realized that she'd actually given him an open invitation to date her—using about as much finesse as a well-aimed bop with a baseball bat—and he had rebuffed it. She squirmed inwardly. That's what comes of forgetting all the civilized ritual of dealing with boys. You tease and kid and tantalize them. You don't level with them and let them know they'd be welcome—awfully welcome!

Why should it matter so? she cried inwardly, hating herself for being upset. He doesn't mean anything. Just another boy. But it didn't ring true. Joel mattered. For whatever reason, he mattered more than any boy she'd ever known.

She roused to the fact that she must have come quite a way. She felt as if time had been brushed away with the wind. The gusts were quickening, ripping at her roughly—no sleek airstream such as had poured around her when the T-Bird hit its pace. This was a ragged blast that shook her. It was getting colder, too. She felt tired all at once, as though she'd been walking for hours.

Climbing the bank of the ravine, she winced at the harsh sweep of the gale up there on the flat. A thick curtain of sand was sheeting across the desert; the air was threaded with it, the sun only a dim yellow spot overhead. Through the haze she made out the station, far back, the little huddle of buildings almost lost to view. The torrent of air was buffeting her so that she had to take shelter again in the gulch.

Crouching in the lee of one rocky wall, she managed to scrub her eyes clear enough to see again, though they felt seared. It was a question now of how to get home. The wash meandered like a snake—it would take hours to follow it back. Christie was shivering hard in the thin cotton shirt; each gust seemed to come colder. Straight across land would be quickest, but she didn't think she could beat her way into the wind up there.

Crawling up the embankment again, she shielded her eyes with her hands, but it was no use. She was driven back before she could even attempt to scramble out on top.

It was obvious that she'd walked out into a Santa Ana. A little frightened, she turned back down the ravine to retrace her steps, hurrying, for even there the wind flayed her with sand. Rounding a bend, she caught the blast full face and had to turn from it a minute, hiding her eyes. She even had a wild impulse to take shelter under one of the rocks and wait for it to let up, but that was plain foolish. The temperature was still dropping, and if it really was a Santa Ana, it could get worse and stay that way—possibly for days. Berating herself for being stupid and careless, she turned into it again and stumbled along, getting more exhausted every step of the way. The wind even seemed to be playing tricks, sounding like a voice, calling. . . .

"Christie!"

She squinted through her fingers and made out some-one coming along the draw, half running.

"Joel!" she whispered, but the word choked up in her throat and all she could do was hurry on unsteadily to meet him.

As he reached her, a new shock wave caught them, drove them together. He held her tight against the force of it and Christie clung to him, almost limp against the solid support of his arms around her. With her face buried in his shirt front, she thought she heard him speaking brokenly, the words almost lost in the scream of the wind.

". . . the only good thing . . . all these years . . ." he seemed to be mumbling to himself. For an instant his cheek rested against her hair. It almost sounded as though he said, "Help me. . . ."

It took them a while to get their bearings, but finally Joel led her over to a sheltered niche in the wall of the ravine and helped her put on his windbreaker.

"Little dope," he said fondly, "do you always charge off into a storm without even a coat?"

"Only when I'm all in pieces," she said ruefully.

"I know. I did it, with what I said. I felt bad when I saw you walk off that way—I kept watching for you

105

to come back. Then your mother came out looking for you. And Wayne came around to tell us to tie down; the wind's due to hit a hundred and up this afternoon. That's when I really got scared."

"How did you know where to find me?"

"I knew you'd gone down into the wash. I supposed you would walk away from the wind. Mostly I just went on and hoped."

Christie wondered how she could have ever thought of him as remote. Standing here so close, his hands framing her shoulders as if to make sure she was all right, he was as near to her as anyone had ever been.

"If you've caught your breath," he was going on, "we'd better start back. Some of the others are looking, too. We'll head straight across the open and try to get home as soon as possible, to stop the search."

"What a darned nuisance I turned out to be." She smiled shakily. "Do you think we can make it the hard way?"

He took her hand. "Stay behind me and keep your head down."

"It'll take the skin off you!" she protested, glancing at his threadbare shirt sleeves.

"Got to try it." He helped her up the bank into the world of the storm and swinging her in close behind him, led the way into the wind.

They seemed to flounder along endlessly over fields of black rock and through soft spots of sand. Sometimes Christie was kept on her feet only by the clasp of his fingers holding her up, urging her along. She lost track of where they were, but Joel, with his free arm up to shield his face, plowed ahead steadily. About halfway back to camp they spotted Wayne Slater.

He came up grinning—the first time Christie had ever seen him look pleased. "Nice day to go walking!" he shouted. Then slapping Joel's shoulder, he added, "Good thing you found her. This baby's getting worse. Pedro's gone up the wash. I'll go bring him back."

Joel nodded. "Anybody else?"

"No. McKinney's trying to brace his trailer. I don't know where Burnett is, and I don't care—the ornery cuss!" The gale carried his voice away as he left them.

Stella's eyes were red—she said it was from the sand. Nervously, happily, she kept dabbing at things as she hovered around the living room while Christie, bundled in a warm robe, sat on the couch and drank some hot tea. She was coming out of the shock of the storm, but hadn't quite recovered from the surprise of finding Burnett here in their living room, calmly occupying Dad's easy chair.

The room seemed small and snug against the racket of the wind. Their seclusion here together, with the lanterns making a small comfortable hissing, had a flavor of intimacy that made Christie uncomfortable. She couldn't help picturing Dad's consternation if he were to walk in right now and find Mom entertaining this subversive character.

Burnett was maddeningly at ease. "Too bad Joel wouldn't join us," he remarked, speaking to Stella, though his look was on Christie.

Mom was filling teacups that didn't need filling. "Such a nice boy! He said he was needed to help Mr. Moreno and the others brace their trailers. So thoughtful. So *polite*. In fact, everybody's been just wonderful, going off into this terrible wind—"

"Not everybody went off into it," murmured Christie, squeezing some lemon into her tea.

Burnett smiled, understanding her completely.

Mom looked at her anxiously. "But, Kitty, it was a good thing somebody stayed around the court. You should have seen how this trailer was rocking, like a little boat in the ocean. I was so frightened—you out there and the house about to go over. It's just lucky Mr. Burnett came along and propped it with the—the—what-you-call-its."

"Angle irons. However, I'd have to disagree about the luck of it." He took some of his drink, handling Mom's best china as adeptly as he did everything else. "I've never found it safe to rely on luck. When the wind first started, I hunted up those lengths of iron, just in case. I've been in Santa Anas before and I'm pessimistic about them."

"Well, what I mean"—Mom flurried over and offered him some more sugar—"is that it was lucky you stayed around the court."

Burnett shook his head. "That wasn't luck either."

108

"What was lucky," Christie remarked moodily, "was that somebody found me out in all that mess of nowhere. If Joel hadn't guessed right—"

"Do you really think that was luck?" Burnett asked innocently. "I'd say it was natural law. I'm a strong believer in that. When I saw the young man start out, I had every faith in the powers of gravitation."

Christie wondered whether he wasn't laughing at her. Mom took it as humor. She smiled, misty-eyed.

"Whatever it was, I'm grateful." Coming over to the couch, she snuggled down close beside Christie as if to reassure herself all over again. "And all the time, Kitty, Mr. Burnett was soothing me. I really did need soothing. Just as he said, I was getting like a smoky bottle."

"A what?" Christie choked a little on the hot tea.

Burnett set the fragile cup down and stood up. "I'm glad to have been of service, and now I'm going to leave before things get spoiled."

"Spoiled—how?" Mother looked up at him in dismay.

"I don't know how." For the first time he spoke without the least trace of mockery. "I really don't. But there's definitely a time to stay and a time to go."

"And a time to come back."

He shook his head. "I doubt that." Something in his tone brought to Christie's mind that remark of the Señora's about Burnett being lonely. Stella evidently got some inkling of it, too, for as she got up to go to the door with him, she spoke with surprising firmness.

"Oh, yes, Mr. Burnett. I want you to come back."

11

Sam Ford stood in the middle of the living room, watching helplessly as Stella surrounded him. She was in the kitchen one minute, helping Christie mix the turkey dressing; back up to the front window making sure the bland sunny day was still beautiful; then over to the tree to arrange a piece of tinsel; pausing by the pile of newly opened Christmas presents to gloat over the book on gardening.

"Don't you think you ought to get the fire started, Sam?" she asked as she trotted back to the kitchen. "The turkey is almost ready to cook, and I asked everybody for two o'clock."

"Slater's going to build the fire," he answered vaguely.

"He knows how to roast over an open pit and I don't. You know, Stella, you really ought to consider my limitations before you launch on something like this."

"You don't have any limitations, pet." Mom came and handed him a carton of eggs. "You make the best eggnog in the state of California."

"Have you considered what we'll all talk about?" he demanded, pacing up to the front window with the eggs still gripped in his hand. As he looked out at the row of trailers, you could see him trying to imagine how those human ingredients were going to mix in the shaker.

"Burnett, too." He shook his head, set the eggs down on the window sill and came back. "I tell you, Stella, water and oil don't mix."

"Oh, Sam. I'm sure Mr. Burnett will be quite able to wash all the oil off before he comes!" She tittered at her own joke.

"That's not what I mean and you know it. Just because he did what was evidently necessary in that storm —and I certainly credit him for coming to your assistance—all the same, it doesn't mean he'll be a—a—social asset."

"It wasn't the iron things that steadied me that day." Stella paused long enough to look across at her husband with rare defiance. "It was the way he talked. He said some very sensible things. I'm sure he'll be very interesting to have at the dinner."

"He called Mom a smoky bottle," Christie added.

"Not exactly. He quoted something. I forget how it

111

went, but part of it was 'I am like a bottle in the smoke.' And that's exactly how I felt right then."

"Probably some beatnik poetry," Dad said glumly.

"It sounded more like Scripture. Anyhow, Mr. Burnett is human, and I just wanted to bring everybody together and do something nice for them after they were all so kind. Anyhow, it's settled, they're coming, so do make the eggnog, Sam."

Sighing, Dad went over to the cabinet where the glassware was kept and started to get out the punchbowl and cups. Stopping abruptly, he stared at the row of planters on top of the cabinet. Long since vacant of African violets, they had suddenly sprouted a new full-grown feathering of greenery.

"What—in the—name of—heaven!" he marveled. "Those pots were empty when I left for L. A. How did you get anything to come up in this length of time?"

Mom came over to his side, pleased. "Those are my carrots. I do like fresh carrots."

He stared still, as if unwilling to believe his eyes. "I always knew you were a good gardener, Stella, but to produce full-grown carrots in ten days—!"

She smiled over the plants. "I didn't exactly 'produce' them; I bought them last Friday. They were so little and sweet, and I managed to get them before Mabel had put them in the refrigerator. So I brought them right home and planted them in some sand. They do best in sand, and goodness knows there's plenty of it around. Look, this one's even putting out a new leaf." She grew sober and

112

wondering. "I'm going to hate to pull them up."

Dad brought the punchbowl over to the sink. For the first time in weeks he was grinning.

The eggnog seemed to have warmed the men toward each other that afternoon. They grouped around the roasting pit like a klotch of top chefs while the women fitted together an assortment of tables into one big banquet board. On the odd-shaped object strange linens rubbed hems with each other: Mom's cutwork bridge cloth next to Mrs. Moreno's red cotton. Mrs. McKinney had contributed a plastic monstrosity, noisy with blue chrysanthemums. Mabel had brought paper napkins— one to a person.

Christie doled them out at each plate, resisting an impulse to giggle. Trying to keep sober, she thought she should darn well be taking tips in hostessing; Mom had actually drawn Mrs. McKinney and Mabel into a discussion that was at least neutral if not exactly chummy. Apparently they did have one interest in common after all—the guck that plastered their faces. Mrs. McKinney's fat, rouged cheeks worked up and down and Mabel batted her mascara-laden lashes as each tried to out-know the other on brands and trade names. That left Stella free to talk to Señora Moreno. Mom had obviously been dying to get her hands on the baby, who sat quiet, clutching the new doll and staring round-eyed at the fire.

Having finished the table setting, Christie picked up a plate of appetizers and moved toward the circle of men.

113

They seemed to be getting on fairly well. Dad had just waved his eggnog cup, which was a good sign. Only Joel stood a little removed, talking no part in the talk.

As she drifted around the outskirts, Christie gathered that the subject was taxes.

". . . I have a few extra 1040 forms," Dad was saying. "If you like, Mr. Moreno, I'll show you how to fill one out. But you can rest assured you don't owe any tax."

The little Mexican's face shone with relief. "I think maybe I get a new clutch then."

"Me, I consider it a privilege to pay taxes to the good old U. S.," McKinney announced with random truculence. "If there's one thing I hate it's a germ that wiggles out of paying taxes. The rest of us just have to carry 'em, like leeches." He stared so squarely at Burnett that the redheaded man had to field the ball.

Easily he said, "Oh, I pay my dues every April, too. Even though I sometimes deplore the necessity when I think of the portion spent on road construction, where freeloaders sit around broadening their backsides on my money."

McKinney flushed hotly and would have retorted if Slater hadn't looked up sharply from tending the fire. "Cut it out, you guys," he said. "This is a party."

"Turkey smells pretty good," ventured one of the old men—Charlie Sheets, who lived in the front trailer.

Christie had been careful not to notice the fact that he and the other old-timer, Gabe, had cleaned up the whole plateful of appetizers. The way they had gone at it, they

114

must have been starving for little, different flavors.

The curious part was that Joel was so attentive to them. He saw to it that they had comfortable chairs at the table and poured their coffee out of the big enamel pot, as if anticipating that it would be too heavy for their arthritic old hands. It was done unnoticeably, while the others were all milling around the table, finding places, and Dad was beginning to serve.

When the others were all settled, Christie caught Joel's eye; he got the message, came around and took the seat she'd saved. They had spent some wonderful days together since the storm—warm, friendly hours of a sort of companionship that didn't really need much talk to hold it together. Of course, they had talked, but only of impersonal things—things that didn't matter. Joel was avoiding the important subjects, trusting her to avoid them, too. If she sometimes got a rankling little feeling that something was hanging over them, it was easy enough to put it away from her. Just the touch of his hand on her arm was enough to make her forget the whole world.

And she had no doubt, now, that it was mutual. Sometimes she was curiously unsettled by the full-grown masculine appreciation of his look. It had registered swiftly when she had stepped out into the patio this afternoon, dressed in a simple, white silk jersey. He himself had dug up a suit shiny with age, one that she suspected had belonged to somebody else. And yet as she sat beside him she wouldn't have traded places with anyone on earth. The fullness of this feeling was so new, she could hardly define it.

At the far end of the table Stella, ruffly as a hollyhock in her pink chiffon dress, was trying to keep the conversation flowing shallow and safe.

"Has everybody seen the lovely doll that Joel made for the baby's Christmas present?" she remarked, to get things going.

"Joel *made* this doll?" Dad asked, shocked. Mrs. Moreno was seated at his right, with the sleeping infant on her lap.

"Just the head, sir," the boy said quickly. "That dress is the real work of art."

Christie, too, had marveled at the elegance of the costume that the Señora had fashioned out of old silk and delicate lace to clothe the soft rag body of the doll.

"I take from my marriage dress," the Señora told them. "Is good for the baby to hold something beautiful."

So then the doll had to be passed around in order that they all could see.

"Reminds me of the toys they used to make years ago," commented old Gabe wistfully. "Some of them was handsome."

Stella agreed enthusiastically. "And they were all different! The silly faces you see on the ones in the stores these days—well, they just don't warm you! I wonder why there's never any character to them any more."

"Because that takes imagination and skill," Burnett

116

told her, looking down at the doll, which had come to him. "This kind of craftsmanship is almost a lost art. Have you done it professionally, Joel? How did you learn it?"

Christie felt the boy go tense, just as he had once before when she'd asked the same question.

"I just picked it up," he said.

Burnett glanced at him in sharp disbelief and passed the doll on. It came around to Sam Ford again, who looked at it all over, still openly astounded. "Shows talent. My boy, you could turn this into money. As Mr. Burnett says, handwork comes high these days."

Joel shook his head. "If you find anybody who wants it. Most companies use machines. The toys don't turn out so well, but they're cheaper. Anybody can learn to run a machine."

"Oh, is that so?" McKinney scowled. "Well, I got one answer for you guys that knock machinery. I say, okay, you take a spade and I'll get on a dragline and we'll see who can fill a ten-yard truck faster."

"I didn't say I was against machinery," Joel denied uncomfortably.

"He just meant," Burnett said, "that he'd rather pick cotton than push buttons."

"I didn't say that either!"

"However," the redhead went on imperturbably, "you ought to at least consider automation for its virtues as a painkiller. You get nicely seated behind a bunch of levers and your mind and body go soft together.

117

Maybe you should try it, Joel. Because as long as you stick to the fields and use your muscles, you'll still find yourself thinking. And that's doing things the hard way, you'll admit."

Joel ducked his head over his plate and ate.

"You calling me soft?" McKinney bridled, all unaware of any other undercurrents. "Bud, any time you want to be took on—"

"Cynicism aside," Dad put in quickly, "I think Joel could make out well in Los Angeles. As a matter of fact, I know some people who might be interested in getting a young man of your ability, my boy. If you'd like an introduction—"

"Thank you, sir," Joel murmured. "It's just—well, I don't want to work for anybody. I'm doing okay, I'm my own boss."

Burnett looked aggrieved. "That's a booby trap, boy. Mr. Ford would be the first to tell you so."

Dad gave Mom a look that meant: How much did you tell this hobo that day he was propping up the trailer?

Stella rallied weakly to his support. "Why, Mr. Burnett, don't tell us you're against free enterprise?"

"Of course not, ma'am. I'd be very interested in it, if it were available. I haven't ever run into any that was free."

"Listen, you!" McKinney's jaw was beginning to jut out in Burnett's direction. "Any time you don't like our good old country you can leave. Nobody'll miss you."

118

The redheaded man considered this mildly. "I think they might. If everybody who doesn't agree were to run off, there'd be no enlightened opposition. Don't you believe in a two-party system, Mac?"

"Oh, dear, let's don't talk politics!" Stella pleaded.

"I'll ask you just one thing." McKinney pointed a finger at Burnett. "Did you or didn't you vote in the last election?"

"Nope." The hobo sighed. "Couldn't."

"HA!" Mac shouted triumphantly. "I knew it! There's only one type of citizen can't vote and that's bums with a police record."

"Wrong again." Burnett smiled. "The other disenfranchised legion are we who commit the error of moving from one community to another. You—me—Mr. Ford, all in the same boat. Unless we abide here through the heat of summer, the state of California, which is no worse than most, will judge us ineligible to take part in the choosing of a President next fall."

"Well, for the love of—!" Ford exploded. "I came out here for my health! A man ought not to be penalized for that! It's a damnable law that isn't flexible enough to take into account certain circumstances."

"I'm afraid a lot of laws step on various people's circumstances," Burnett said coldly. "Must be ridiculously easy to pass a law these days. Last year alone saw over twenty-eight thousand new 'Thou shalt nots' go on the books. No wonder the younger generation has an impulse to buck all the restrictions and controls. Or if not

119

buck them, hide out from them." He glanced at Joel keenly.

Dad was still fuming about having lost his right to vote. "By Harry, I'm going to write my congressman about this!"

"Won't do any good," Burnett told him. "There aren't enough of us pilgrims to make a good lobby. We're not even constituents of anything. We're on one of the lost stretches in the maze of civilized living. But it could be worse. Think of the kids, just coming up to the starting point, wondering which turnoff will lead them into a dead end. . . ."

Mom dropped her fork with a clatter. When they looked at her, she smiled with visible determination.

"Pie, anybody?"

As they stood around getting ready to leave, telling the Fords how good the supper had been, Christie was vividly conscious of Joel standing silent beside her. She knew he was waiting for the others to go, that he wanted to be alone with her. She knew he was disturbed.

But why had he kept so still through all the talk at the table? Burnett's words had been like a rasp, raising the grain on everybody. Nobody would have blamed Joel if he'd answered back to the jibing.

And when the redhead had spoken of laws, Christie had practically tasted the hot words of rebellion. You want to know what young people think? We think it's a bind! We think everything's so complicated, you're cut off before you begin! Sure, we wish we could hide from them, or unmake them or something. Except that laws never get unmade, even the ones that grownups hate, too.

And yet Joel hadn't said any of it. He'd kept still and let Mom drag the conversation back into frivolities. Now they were all leaving, with the usual bland compliments.

"It may be a little premature," Sam Ford was saying, "but I wish you all a happy new year."

"Thanks, fella, same to you and many of 'em." McKinney yawned.

Burnett said, "Mr. Ford, I appreciate your optimism, even if I can't subscribe to it."

For some reason Wayne Slater, who had just downed the last of the leftover eggnog, was suddenly rubbed wrong. In a flare of anger he turned on Burnett.

"Who are you to bellyache?" he demanded. "All day you been singing sour. Man, it's Christmas! It's the first day I closed the station since last Christmas and I don't feel like worrying. I worry enough the rest of the time. If a guy says it's gonna be a happy new year, I'll punch any buzzard that says it's not."

"Wayne, you're just suffering from too much 'free' enterprise," Burnett told him helpfully. "If you worry so much, why not close up every day—go on off and pick cotton with Joel?"

The boy went red with sudden anger. "I don't know what you're trying to prove, Burnett, but that's the second time you've jeered at a man for trying to get along under his own power. Seems like you're petty anxious to convince everybody that no matter where they want to go, they can't get there from here. What Wayne does or what I do is none of your business."

"Of course it's my business." All at once Burnett wasn't kidding. He looked hard as a judge. "I expect to live in this land for some time to come. I've got a right to worry what will happen to it when the people your age take it over—or aren't you planning to help with the job?"

"It's your generation running it now," Joel came back. "So where do you figure in the scene? What's your contribution, Burnett?"

The hobo didn't try to evade the challenge. He met the boy's look thoughtfully and took his time answering.

"I serve a purpose," he said at last. "But before you can question it, you've got to get out of the cotton field."

12

Together Christie and Joel walked away from the court in the early twilight of the Christmas afternoon; neither tried to talk. The overtones of the heated exchange of words still rang in the girl's ears, sharply clear against the hush of the desert.

It was a breathless evening; the earth was still as a picture painted in water color with long sweeps of the brush—umbrous sands trimmed by distant black rimrock heights; pale gray sky; and far off to the west some high streamer of sunset caught two jet trails, brilliant pink gold, going away. . . .

Joel was heading for one of the outcroppings of rock that thrust up through the floor of sand not far from the court. They climbed the ragged pile; it put them only a dozen feet above the desert, but even that felt high and somehow remote.

He spread his windbreaker for Christie to sit on, but he himself stood for a minute looking back toward the highway where headlights strung out like small stars moving in a long path across the diameter of the empty land.

The quiet stretched out. And yet with Joel beside her, Christie didn't mind it. It was a relief after Burnett's merciless questioning. All the goading, prying, demanding—Christie hoped fervently it hadn't driven Joel back into the shell that had held him so unreachable at first.

"I hate grownups," she murmured, without thinking —just coming out loud with an old ache.

Joel shook off his thoughts. "You hate what?"

"Adults. People like Burnett, the big bully. They're all the same. What gives them the right to put us on the griddle?"

Joel smiled whimsically. "I haven't thought of people as 'adults' for so long—"

Christie swallowed a small lump of sheepishness; she felt as if she'd just been caught with her pinafore showing.

"What I mean is," she amended lamely, "people are always riding other people. And if you try to pin *them* down they dodge or put you off."

"Look, Christie"—Joel sat down beside her—"I don't like Burnett, but this was a fair argument. He said some-

124

thing I didn't like and I told him so. He asked me a question I wouldn't answer; he had a right not to answer mine."

"But he started it all!"

"That's his privilege, too, I guess. What I don't get is his own attitude. If he's so worried about the world, why doesn't he do something about it instead of trying to discourage other people? What good did it do to make Wayne feel like a fool for trying to run his gas station? That made me sore."

"I know. I was wondering why you got mad at that particular thing."

"Because Wayne's a helpless character. He's scared— always on the verge of going broke. If he gets feeling low it may push him over the edge." Some emotion that lay deep beneath the quick-spoken words seemed out of proportion. Christie didn't understand it, but it frightened her.

"All that talk about wandering in a maze, coming to a dead end," he went on restlessly. "What was the point in reminding the poor beat old men that they're stuck and helpless? They really are. For good. But why keep driving it home?" He broke off and seemed to realize that he'd been talking to her, not just to himself. "I'm sorry. I didn't mean to get teed off."

"But I think it's wonderful," she said, bewildered, "that you care about all those others."

"It isn't," he answered almost curtly. "It's a drag, feeling sorry for people. I'd like to hate Burnett, for

125

being so right—everybody at the party today, everybody in this camp, just stumbling around, wondering which turn to take, and he makes sport of it. What does he want us to do, go jump off a bridge?"

Christie shivered a little. In instant apology Joel put an arm across her shoulders lightly, a gesture so protective and yet full of his own need that Christie wanted to return it in kind. It was hard to sit close and steady, just giving as much support as he would accept.

"Don't you think," she said cautiously, "that most things kind of—work themselves out?"

"No, I don't! If a man can't take care of himself and come up with the right answers, how can he ever have anybody rely on him, like a family? You think *they* can just be left to luck? Nobody else is going to take care of them for you. So if you don't think there are very many right answers—" Again he broke off short as if every twist of conversation did bring him against a blank wall.

Christie felt strangely afraid. A thought of Rudy flashed across her mind—just a freewheeling character who wouldn't worry. About anything. He might smash himself up in that T-Bird someday and not even worry about that. He seemed awfully little, as she thought back. This one, so close beside her, was a man, with a man's troubles, and by his face and tone of voice she knew they were grim.

At last Joel stirred impatiently. "I shouldn't have got to talking; talk just strings me up right now. The real reason I asked you to come out here was that I have something for you." He felt in the pocket of his coat and brought out a small package.

Christie took it shyly. "Joel, I didn't expect a Christmas present."

"It isn't, particularly. This is just from me to you." He glanced at the sky where the stars had come out with sudden brilliance, as if they'd just been flung in handfuls across the silk-blue night. "I guess there's light enough to see."

She unwrapped the box, took out a small silver buckle. In her palm it shone almost with a radiance of its own; a narrow rectangle with a slight flare, a delicate tongue, rich in its simplicity.

"It's beautiful!" she whispered.

"I hope you'll like it in daylight, too," he said, with a touch of deprecation. "You'll see where it could have been improved. I'm not so good at engraving as I ought to be."

"You carved this yourself!"

"I had to try to make you something good that would be just right for you. The belt you wear is nice leather, but the buckle is just like all the others in the world."

"But—silver? Joel!"

"I could be put in jail for that." He laughed. "There's a law against whittling on coins. I carved that out of a silver dollar. But the dollar wouldn't have bought me enough flat stock to make a buckle and I wanted pretty badly to make it."

Holding it clenched tight in her hand, Christie burst out impulsively, "Joel, if you can make a beautiful thing like this, there shouldn't be anything ever for you to worry about! This is different and wonderful, and I love it! Other people would love it!"

"That's beside the point." He shook his head help-lessly. "You don't know—I'm glad you don't know." Reaching out, he touched her cheek, stroked her hair back away from her face. Then he drew her to him and kissed her—a hard embrace that had a desperation in it.

Dizzied by the rush of emotion it brought, Christie was distantly aware that this was no easy-come gesture for him. Joel hadn't kissed many girls.

Releasing her, he got up and walked off a step or two. "I didn't mean to do that."

"I—didn't either," she stammered. "But it's all right —everything's all right."

"No, everything's wrong, except you." He held out a hand to help her up. "Someday when you're ready for it you'll be all a man could ever want. You try to help, you care about things. You'll warm him, you'll never let him get downhearted." Joel spoke fiercely, as though something were tormenting him. "But I had no right to start this. We shouldn't be here. We've got to go back right now."

Silently they went down the slope together. Joel found the footing; Christie followed. His last words had put him a million miles away again, and she knew she

128

must not even try to close the distance just then.

But I will, she cried inwardly. *I'll find some way!*

Christie slept uneasily that night. Certain words kept echoing through her dreams. "All a man could want . . . I had no right . . ."

With the abruptness of premonition she wakened some time deep into the morning. Beyond the window a faint band of gray showed in the east. Starting up with the frightened sense of having slept too long, she gathered the nightgown around her and rushed softly, barefoot, into the front room, over to the window, where she was brought up short. For a long time she stood staring helplessly—hopelessly—at the vacant spot across the court where Joel's trailer had stood.

13

Stricken with a kind of numbness, Christie moved about that morning, doing some sort of chores. She felt as if she had to keep moving or fold up. She didn't let herself think much until— When Pete came to her out in the middle of the court, she had to listen.

". . . and on account of he left so sudden, Joel said I should tell you I can put the buckle on the belt for you. I know pretty good how to do with leather. He say he's sorry he couldn't do it before he leave."

"Where did he go?" she asked woodenly. "Did he tell you?"

"Over Arizona. He been pretty low on cash. Got a card from the employment last week, some cotton come in down around Phoenix. He told me not to say—like it would spoil the Christmas party." Pete's brown face was full of sympathy. "Don't worry. Joel makes out okay, I think. He works hard. Get some money pretty quick."

"Will he be back?" She had to ask, even though she was afraid to hear the answer.

Pete shook his head. "Didn't say. He been in a hard time lately. I don't know—"

She nodded blindly and walked on. But the protective layer of shock was ripped aside and the whole reality of it began to throb like pain after a sudden cut. Worse still, that old pounding tightness that had beat so hard inside her, weeks before, came back in a rising tide. Her steps quickened. She had to escape that; she just couldn't go back to that. Past the station she went, onto the railroad tracks, hurrying, overstepping some of the crossties.

Far out ahead she saw a train coming, its weird electric eye swinging crazily, glittering against the bright day— an arrogant, leering thing, ordering her to get off the track. Everybody always pushing you around, shoving you aside. She had an angry impulse to charge headlong at it. But, as the diesel loomed nearer, her defiance faltered and she scuffed down the embankment into a small arroyo, where she stumbled over to the shade of some branchy little trees, the ironwood that Joel—

Sinking onto the cool sand, she covered her face with her hands. How does a boy come to mean so much? Just because his eyes quicken when he looks at you?

131

Because he held you steady against the wind? Or was it that he seemed to need steadying himself last night when he kissed you?

Above, the train burst past with a shriek of whistle that almost broke Christie in two. The rattle and clang of it pounded inside her like the pulse she was so afraid of—it seemed to race faster and faster, until abruptly the last car whipped past, trailing a wake of silence. And Christie, face still hidden in her hands, realized that she had held together.

Grief was just a low fire burning in her. This was no kin to the destructive acid that had almost eaten through the nerve fibers in those days before she came to the desert. That was something done with, gone for good, even though she couldn't have explained why.

Raising her head, she blinked. For a split second, she thought she was seeing an illusion, the man standing there blended so subtly with the bright sun-struck sand. Burnett smiled.

"Good girl. I can see there was no need for me to worry this time."

"Do you make a career out of popping up in the middle of nowhere?" Christie didn't really want to talk to him. She just wanted to sit here alone and mourn for Joel.

"Sorry. I didn't mean to sneak up on you. The train must have covered my footsteps." His manner was so genuinely kind, she couldn't stay irritated. In fact, some new gentleness of tone intrigued her. "I saw you head out of camp," he went on. "You looked a trifle uneven,

132

so I thought I'd follow along, just in case."

"In case what?"

Burnett sat down on a flat rock near her. "I may be wrong, but a couple of times I thought I saw the seams start to split. That first day we talked, I could have sworn you were on the verge of a bad case of nerves."

Christie blurted out honestly, "I was!" It brought a flood of relief, to be able to speak of it. "That's why we came to the desert. But Mom and Dad don't know that I know—" It poured out, the whole story; Burnett listened attentively.

"That explains a lot," he said when she'd finished. "Especially as concerns your parents. They've had me puzzled. I've been particularly worried about your mother—quite a remarkable woman."

"Mom's been calmer ever since you quoted the beatnik poetry about the smoky bottle," Christie told him with faint humor.

Burnett didn't smile; for the first time since she'd known him, he looked shocked. "Who told you it was 'beatnik'?"

"My father. He was just guessing, of course; Mom didn't really remember the words."

"I'm sorry for that. She may need them again someday, although her problems are somewhat different from yours. She knows what the score is, she just hasn't been given much chance to run the bases. All in all, I'd say your father's probably the one to worry about right now."

"You can't do anything for Dad," she assured him.

133

"He won't talk about things—even to Mom and me."

"And there you have the mischief," murmured Burnett. Absently he pulled an orange from his pocket, offered it to Christie. "The yeast of honest words is sometimes enough to start a whole brew of solutions working. And yet people are afraid of it. Joel is. I was hoping maybe last evening you'd be able to draw him out, in private." He broke off. "Here, let me peel that for you."

Christie gave up fumbling with the orange and watched while he went about it deftly. "No, I didn't have any luck. But then he was very upset. You were awfully mean the way you rode him. Why do you sometimes treat people kindly and then again you needle?"

"That's a good question." He broke the orange in sections and handed it back. "A needle is a handy tool at times. I firmly believe there's a time to rend and a time to sew. But my remarks weren't what sent the boy off. In fact, for a minute there he was almost all right. I was quite disturbed to find he'd vanished off into the desert this morning. I'd hoped you had averted it."

"He needed money."

"I know that. But there are better ways to get it than picking cotton. Of course, maybe he's headed for something better."

"No. Pedro says he's on his way to Arizona." Bleakly she said, "I guess he *likes* to pick cotton."

Burnett made a small negative sound. "Ever try it? I

134

have. For two days once, which was all I could take. Made thirteen dollars and fifty cents for twenty-nine hours of the hardest work I ever did. You sling a long bag around your neck and go along the rows bent double, grabbing the stuff out of the seedpods, which are about as charitable as torn tin cans. The peculiar punishment of the job lies in the fact that the more tired you get, the heavier the sack is growing as you keep shoving the fluff into it. They don't pay you until you stagger back with a hundred pounds. Oh, I guess they let the children come to the scales with less, but not the men. After you finish a day of that you can lie right down on a bare board floor and fall asleep."

Christie could hardly swallow the piece of orange. "I wish you hadn't told me."

"You're no baby. You've got to know what Joel's been going through before you'll ever be able to get to him." He spoke commandingly. "And for heaven's sake don't get into a state of nerves again."

Christie's chin came up. "Do you think I want to? But how should I know what brings it on? I didn't ever know to begin with."

"Why, that's obvious!" Then Burnett checked. "No, I guess it's never obvious to the one caught up in it. Have you ever considered the nature of laws? Or maybe I should have put that the other way around, the laws of . . ."

"I hate laws!" she broke in vehemently. "I don't want to think about laws."

135

"Oh." He stood up. "I thought you wanted to understand what was ailing you."

"What do laws have to do with it?"

"Just this: That you do not hate them. If you're normal, you were born needing certain ones. Unfortunately, some of the man-made variety get unreasonable and the very number of them confuses you, as to which are good and which aren't, so you think you resent them. But just consider what you feel when you break one— even a petty ordinance like jaywalking or cutting school. Doesn't it give you a simmer of unrest, a precarious feeling of loss of rhythm or balance, at least for a few minutes? You must know what I'm talking about. So consider the upset that happens when you go against the bigger ones—the laws that make the manufactured variety look like silly doodling."

Baffled as she was by the words, the intensity with which he spoke wakened some odd response in Christie. He'd put a finger on something she had felt down deep, a sense of being off balance, out of timing.

"But what one did I break?" she asked, perplexed.

"Look here." He hunkered down in the sand and ran his fingers through the green plant life that still thrived stubbornly after all these weeks. "Something powerful governs this. Could you deny it? But suppose the little things tried deliberately to quit growing? Or suppose somebody convinced them they'd look better if they turned blue? Well, of course, you've turned back to your natural color so you'll probably be all right from

136

now on. But Joel—I'm afraid he's trying to break the biggest law of all." He grew silent and troubled.

"What—?" she began, but he waved the question off.

"If you can't figure it out, you can't help him when he comes back."

"What makes you think he'll be back?" Christie started to follow Burnett up the bank, but he stopped her with a shake of the head.

"If I were you, dear child, I'd shun my nefarious company, at least in public, unless you want another batch of words from your father. Stay here in the shade and try to concentrate. I hope you come to some conclusions. For Joel's sake."

"But if I could, how do you know I'll have a chance to—"

Burnett stood, one foot on the track, looking down at her. "I told you I never leave anything important to chance. I was fairly sure the boy was planning to take off when he asked me to grease his old bucket and change the oil. That antique burns oil like a furnace. So I thought I'd better make sure he'd come back."

"How?"

"I loaned him fifty dollars. If I know Joel, he'll drive a long way to pay money back to a man he doesn't like."

"I wouldn't think he'd have accepted it!"

"Oh, he wouldn't." Burnett smiled. "That's why I took the precaution to wrap it in an envelope around the oil stick. He'll discover it about sixty miles out. He can't send me a money order. He doesn't even know my right

137

name, a fact which I was at pains to point out the other day. And he'd not be fool enough to send cash, not even knowing whether I'd still be here. No, he'll be back to return it in person. And by then you'd better have your course well planned, my dear—I doubt if you'll have much time."

PART
III

Burnett

14

One morning in early February there were birds everywhere. As Christie lay in bed, she heard them calling to each other from somewhere near, two short notes and a long, as if they were crying "Christmas Eve . . . Christmas Eeeve . . ."

After lunch, as she did the dishes unhurriedly, she saw one of the little migrators tilting and bobbing on a brittle arm of the dead bush below the window—a gray bird with a precise black stripe across his wings. Wistfully he called, "Christmas Eve . . ." and the answer came from a long way off, out in the land to the north. Beyond the faraway mountains clouds were piled like blanket rolls. All week they had spread a thick layer over the sky, shredding in spots to send streamers of rain across the desert. Now they were retreating northward, leaving the sky as if it had been polished. A fresh warmth was in the south breeze, enough to bring this flight of new birds.

And the field workers. Now that the spring rains had ended and the cotton season was over, the pickers would be on the move again. With a twinge Christie thought of Joel—or rather the thought that was always there swept forward and swamped her with longing. Every day that passed had added to the misery of waiting.

She glanced at the calendar above the sink. How many hundred pounds of cotton do you drag along the rows in thirty-nine days? She tried to make herself stop thinking about it. Burnett had said to plan, but she wasn't that kind. She couldn't just make up some line of action to take, not with Joel.

Besides, there was a more immediate crisis looming, she was afraid; in fact, it was sitting right out there in the patio now in the person of two unhappy people. And this problem was one hundred per cent hers.

Hanging up the dishtowel, she went outside. Everything just as it had been for a month—this century of a month! Mom was sitting at the card table, poised over the tumbled pieces of a jigsaw puzzle. She'd grown more and more subdued as Dad had got soggier. He'd been worse ever since last week when he'd taken another trip to Los Angeles, this time without even bothering over an excuse. Now, slumped in the folding chair hour after hour, he was obviously being deadened by something.

142

Christie wished acutely that she could help, but neither she nor Mom had been able to pry it out of him. He just sat there, staring blankly, answering them in monosyllables, mostly just listening to the portable radio they'd given him for Christmas. The way he kept switching back and forth, from station to station, reminded Christie of Rudy. The only time Dad even made an attempt to look alive was when McKinney dropped over to chew the rag, as he was doing now—rambling on, nerveless and self-confident.

"All I say is, if you're thinking about going in business for yourself again, you got rocks in your head, Sam. I'm just telling you for your own good. You been doing things the hard way and no joke. You take all the risks, you got all the headaches of keeping the books balanced, you get ulcers trying to outsmart the competition, and what's to show for it? Mostly debts. You know who's got it made?"

"Oh, yes," Ford said dreamily, "Mr. Burnett's got it made. No overhead, no bills to pay, no worries. But I keep wondering—where is he going? What makes him stay alive? There must be some incentive; you don't just live for the sake of the food you eat. Or do you?"

"I don't give a plugged nickel whether he does or don't." McKinney brushed the idea aside. "Like I was going to say, a union man's got it best these days. Draw top pay, don't have to dude up in a white collar. But mainly you can kiss your boss good-by any time he gets smart. Some of these guys, if you aren't running your

143

tail off every minute they think they got to squeeze some more work out of you. That's when I tell 'em where to go. And they can't touch me, either. The union agent can pull every man off a job and the big shots know it. Boy, with a setup like that you can just relax, put in your eight hours the easiest way you can get by with, and sleep every night."

With faint sarcasm Ford said, "Doesn't the monotony of all that goofing bore you a little?"

"Naaa. You learn to pace yourself slow. What I mean is, why kill yourself so some big shot should get rich?"

Christie felt a twinge as she saw the words sink in on Dad. He sat there, gloomy. Because the goof-off was one of the things that had fractured him the worst when he'd been running the shop. Every time he'd had to fire a man, he had come home miserable. He always said it was the financial loss, having to train new employees, that worried him. But Christie had always thought it was mostly his softheartedness.

This past month she'd thought a lot about Dad and the shop. Little half-remembered things kept dropping in place to make a picture a good deal more complex than the jigsaw puzzle that seemed to absorb Mom so much. Christie wished she'd quit fiddling, fiddling endlessly with the garbled pieces of sky and lake and mountain.

Think of the pieces we're in, she urged silently, slouching down on the end of the glider. There was this peculiar feeling that before she could help Joel she'd have to understand her father. However hard to imagine,

144

the fact was that Dad had been Joel's age once. Years ago he had made a chair; back in the days before he had much machinery he'd made this chair—by hand. Reaching back in her memory, she tried to remember what it looked like—sort of shelvy, but there'd been a hint of tender touch to it, a flare almost like the curve of the belt buckle. Christie found herself fingering the little silver ornament unconsciously.

For years it had been Dad's favorite chair. And then somehow it had got lost—sold or given away. She couldn't really remember. And now the whole business was gone, and it was coming clearer to her with every day that Dad was just about heartbroken. Judging by all those week ends he'd spent just puttering around the closed workroom, he must have loved the shop. In spite of taxes and bills, all of his complaining, it must have been the important thing in his life, and to leave it must have been more than just a defeat, as Mom had implied that day—that one day they'd been close and confidential for a moment. Selling out must have been, to Dad, like having a romance break up. It had happened to Christie several times—the "gone" feeling, the loneliness. Although of course now she could realize that those crushes in the early days of high school had been kid stuff compared to the way she felt about Joel.

So actually the situation between Mom and Dad wasn't too different from her own problem with Joel. Both men were bottling it all up inside, as if their women weren't strong enough or smart enough to listen and help. As if they had no business trying. And what was Mom doing about it? Angrily Christie leaned over and put a perfectly obvious section of lake into a vacant spot in the puzzle.

"Thank you, dear," her mother said absently.

McKinney was leaving now, stretching, scratching. ". . . time to take a nap before supper."

After he'd gone, the patio was deathly quiet. At last, out of the stillness, Dad spoke with cold humor, "I believe I once said that McKinney was a man I would hire. He's also a man I'd have to fire. And that is—exactly— why I conked out. There are so many McKinneys."

"Now, Sam, you didn't 'conk' out," Mom denied vigorously. "You sold your business for perfectly legitimate reasons of—"

As if he hadn't heard her, Dad went on. "The fellow was right when he said I've been doing things the hard way. Trying to meet competition, give the buyer an honest break, and maintain a pay roll made up of— McKinneys. It can't be done, I'm afraid. That's why I've just about made up my mind to . . . take a job."

It took them an instant to grasp the news.

"Well," he said irritably, "it must be fairly obvious we can't stay here in never-never land indefinitely. As soon as we're sure my health is improved—"

"What kind of job?" Mom asked anxiously.

"When I was in Los Angeles last week, I looked into the employment picture and found it not particularly bright. Strange how the breeze can shift and a situation

146

begins to smell a bit different. I, myself, made it a policy not to hire a man over forty, and yet now that I find I'm disqualified, time and again, for the same reason, it strikes me that I've never thought myself too old for work. In fact, a man's just beginning to mature—backlog of experience, sense of responsibility, all that. And yet, that's the last thing they ask you. So I can tell you, when I did get an offer I was relieved."

"A good offer?"

"Brown and Bilt need a foreman for their shop."

"A pusher!" Christie gasped. It was the one thing Dad had always refused to have in his own shop—a hired slave driver to crack the whip that he himself wouldn't crack. He always said if men don't want to work, they can't be forced into doing a good job.

"It pays moderately well," Dad was going on brusquely. "Steady income, no worries, no risk."

"But Sam," Stella said, dismayed, "you never liked the Brown and Bilt line. You said it was cheap—"

"Who am I to criticize?" he came back caustically. "At any rate, it's my decision to make. I am considering it seriously—I am thinking about all the aspects. And for the present I'd like to do just that: think. For a while. If you don't mind."

Squelched, Mom looked down at the puzzle, then jumbled it all together impatiently. As she got up to go inside, she looked at Christie, one swift, telling glance in which the girl glimpsed the whole ache of perplexity and

147

helplessness—like a mirror image of her own heart. Somehow it made the two of them allies.

After dinner, going automatically about the last chore of the day—gathering the trash from the wastebaskets—Christie was a million miles off, exploring this new discovery. Her mother knew the score. Burnett had said so, and now she knew it, too. And that still didn't get past the barriers that Dad had set up. He probably thought he was protecting them, when actually he was setting them each apart from the other.

Out on the patio the radio was going; through its limp music she could hear McKinney's nasal small talk. Even the tone of it produced a sort of dread in her, now that she knew what was stewing in Dad's mind. She could hear the union man snickering him deeper into a state of despair that would drive him back to the city, thrust them all into a horrid, tight little future where Dad would hate his work. And Mom—just now Mom had poured a batch of perfectly good chocolate sauce down the drain without even seeming to see what she was doing.

From the distance, McKinney chortled over something. "That's easy . . ."

Christie wanted to rush out and scream at him to go home. Fleetingly she considered the possibility of having a fit of hysterics, was even turning the idea over in her mind as she stepped out into the patio, carrying the basket of trash to be burned.

148

And there a stirring sight startled her out of her plans. Angling in off the highway was a trailer as long as a city block tethered to the rear of a brand-new Cadillac. Like some fantastic visitor from a world she had once read about, it came gliding down the court in silver-and-violet dignity, swung around at the end, and stopped slantwise across three empty trailer spaces. When Christie saw "Beverly Hills" on the license holder, she actually got a lump in her throat.

Swallowing it down, she went on to the end of the court, as she passed this beautiful reminder of a lovely world where life never got raw and money was no worry. For a brief vision she wished vividly that this could be the Fords' world.

The man and woman had got out of the car now; they, too, were silver and violet. The woman's suit was the absolute latest, right off the Miracle Mile, and the man was groomed right out of this dusty world—no doubt about it, a two-shower-a-day man. As Christie went on down into the wash, where the trash burner was, she was thinking that this was the kind of man Dad ought to be rubbing elbows with. It would boost his morale. It might even make him think up some new approaches or something. If there were only some way to get acquainted; Christie was never very good at breaking the ice with new people.

As she stood feeding trash into the burner a little at a time, she was startled to find the elegant woman had come to stand above her on the edge of the ravine. From way up high somewhere she said, "I beg your pardon."

"Yes, ma'am?" Christie beat the fire down a little; it was making smoke right at the lady.

"Does the management permit incineration at all hours?" she asked, very violet.

"You mean this that I'm doing?" Christie smiled. "Just a few papers. I'm sorry it blew your way. I'll be done in a minute."

"Thank you." The woman withdrew.

It had sounded a little haughty, but Christie thought she probably didn't mean it that way. After all, who wants smoke from the ashpit rising in their windows? Putting out the last remnants of fire, she climbed the bank and started back.

By now the whole court was taking inventory of the gleaming yacht that had come to anchor in their harbor. Mabel was standing in the middle of the driveway practically drooling over the Cadillac. Pete and his wife had come out into their yard, which was right next to the rear end of the new trailer; they were staring up at its towering magnificence. Over by the Fords', Mom and Dad and the McKinneys were viewing from a distance. The people had disappeared inside.

Christie went over to join the Morenos. The Señora was carrying the baby in her arms and Christie could never resist the sight of the little hands reaching out for her hair.

"Some job, eh?" murmured Pete with a grin as she came up.

150

"It's terrific, isn't it!"

And then as they stood there together the sound of voices came out to them from the palace on wheels.

"Who were you talking to, Dolly?" the man asked.

Very clearly the woman answered, "One of those dirty pickers. I put a stop to that miserable smoke."

Christie quivered. Taken completely aback, she stared at the others, hardly believing what she'd heard. The Señora was smiling, with an age-old patience.

"Did you hear what that lady said?" choked Christie.

"Lady—?" The Señora shrugged.

It was the kind of thing that had to be thought about awhile. All night Christie had been murky with emotions. She'd hardly slept. But in the cool quiet of daybreak a strange calm came over her. She felt amazingly wide-awake. Getting up, she dressed and slipped out of the trailer.

This wasn't the first time she'd walked out in the dawn. Morning came on so suddenly out here. One minute everything was chiffon gray, with a single morning star hanging brilliant out over the west. Then a rapid spread of light would race across the earth. The modest little gray birds were up ahead of her, scattering away as she moved toward them. Don't rush off, she called after them silently. We're all in this together.

Moving away from the court, she followed a trail that was becoming familiar to her, taking her toward the hillock where she and Joel had spent that last evening.

151

She hadn't climbed it again; something hurt at the thought. But it seemed to draw her near it whenever she went walking. She'd even trodden a path, an easy route that skirted the worst clutters of black rock, the patches of soft sand.

It was good not to be fighting the desert any more. This was no country you could triumph over. It would never be a friendly place to live, but there was something starkly honest about it that she was coming to appreciate. The thorns of the cactus were there in plain sight to be avoided. Not hidden under a Bullocks-Wilshire suit.

Her indignation stirred briefly again, but more in disgust than hurt. She could see, now, that most of her hot embarrassment last evening had been a sort of shame for the woman in the handsome clothes, as a dweller of that world from which Christie herself had come—a world that she had, only moments before, considered beautiful and important. Any emissary from such high places should have shown dignity and tolerance, if nothing warmer. But the arrogant, penetrating words had made Christie want to apologize to the Señora for the whole breed of city cousins who look polished, but turn out to be cheap, plated stuff.

And yet, too, she realized there was really no need to explain or apologize; the Morenos hadn't been hurt. Christie looked down at herself, the crisp yellow shirt and blue jeans still sharp with the crease of the stretcher. If someone calls you "dirty," do you cry—or do you look at yourself and go on breathing?

Suddenly Christie smiled. "Picker," the lady called me. I wish I were that tough. But there are a few things I can do—clean gasoline lanterns, eat canned food when I'm not in the mood for it, make out without television. Maybe I've yet to learn to wash my clothes with a scrubbing brush, but I could do it. My hands wouldn't give out. Not as fast as yours would, ma'am.

And someone said I'd be all a man could want. . . .

Christie stood still as, all at once, in one long reaching stroke, the sun laid a yellow benediction over the earth. For the first time she saw that the greenery was high enough to make its color felt across the grayness of the sand. In the new daylight the desert seemed to come alive. And as Christie stood there, quiet, the scales swung into balance all the way.

15

By the time Christie got back the morning was high. The big trailer was gone and everything seemed back to normal as she walked along the court. But when she entered their own patio, the illusion went up in smoke. Dad was sitting there, burning like a stove. He looked at Christie so hard that he almost seemed unfocused.

"Where've you been?"

"Just out walking."

"Since when?"

"I woke up early. I don't know when it was. Why?"

Mom had come to the door of the trailer. "Now, Sam . . ."

"I know, Stella, I know. But I'm angry. Can't I be angry?"

154

"At me?" Christie asked helplessly.

"No. No, of course not."

"Then what? What happened?"

"It's a situation that will never—be—corrected—until"—Dad was hammering the words as if he were driving a nail—"until that hobo *gets the boot!*"

"Burnett? What's he done?"

"Slater is a fool, a real hundred per cent fool, if he lets this one go by," Dad said grimly, "and by heaven, if he does, we're leaving. That's all. I won't stand still and—"

Christie's heart skidded. "We can't leave now!"

"—and tolerate the presence of a thief in our bosom!"

Christie stared at her mother in anguish. Stella looked unhappy, too.

"The people who were here last night," she explained softly, "had some things—taken. Stolen out of their car. A camera and a pair of binoculars."

"And they think Burnett did it?"

"*I* think Burnett did it," Dad stated furiously, "and unless the tramp is on the road by nightfall, we'll be on the road tomorrow morning."

Christie had been trying to keep clear of Burnett for more reasons than one. Not just the threat of a parental frown, but because of her own confusion. She still hadn't figured out all the curious things he'd said that last time they'd talked; he'd made her feel as if she were only operating on four or five cylinders instead of eight.

Now, though, she simply had to go to him. There was no time to try to solve this one by herself.

She found him alone in the garage. Head bent over the engine of a car, he was holding a long screw driver with the tip against the block, his ear pressed to the handle, eyes closed in concentration, as he listened to the idling of the motor. And so, for a few seconds, Christie stood in the doorway unnoticed.

Relieved of the watchful intensity of his eyes, his face had a beautiful composure. The sensitive mouth was at rest; his finely modeled features, for all their grease smudges, were serene. As she watched him, Christie wondered how Burnett had managed to escape the awful tearing-apart that everybody else seemed to go through.

Straightening at last, he glanced over at her without surprise. "It's mysterious how the least little adjustment of a valve can put the whole works back in tune. But if you don't know how to do it—" Then as he wiped the grease from his hands, he said, "You look perturbed over something, my dear."

"I'm all shook."

"I gather then that you've heard about the excitement you missed an hour ago."

She nodded. "But there's something you don't know. My father thinks—well, never mind what he thinks, but—"

"He thinks I filched the goods, for one thing," Burnett said helpfully. "Is that what's bothering you?"

"Not just that. He says unless Wayne kicks you out

we're going to leave. You'd think it was his camera that got stolen! I don't know why he's acting so wild."

"That's because you weren't here. The man was fairly obnoxious, but when the woman said, 'Where's that yellow-haired girl—' "

"She thought it was me!"

"Didn't your father tell you that?" Irritably Burnett shook his head. "I sometimes wonder how parents ever expect their kids to make sense out of a situation when they withhold half the vital statistics. Yes, to paraphrase it kindly, she suggested that since you were missing from the court, it indicated your guilt. I thought your father was going to pick madam up, in all her splendor, and chuck her into the ashpit. I'd have congratulated him. Unfortunately propriety ruled, and so his fury was— and still is—unrelieved. Once you understand that, you can appreciate why he has to lash out in some direction. I don't mind being the butt."

"Well, I'm not going to let him blame you," Christie said hotly. "I know who the thief is around here, and I'm going to—"

Burnett looked up swiftly, his eyes hard as red agate. "You're going to keep still about it."

Stopped cold, she stared at him in shock. "You mean you know, too?"

"After that incident of the flashlight, I made it my business to find out. What's more important, Slater knows."

Christie gulped. That was the one thing that had held

157

her in check—the terrible embarrassment of having to reveal the truth to Wayne.

"So you see," Burnett went on, "he won't fire me. And your father will not pull out."

"Oh, yes, he will," she moaned weakly. "You just don't know. He's been offered a rotten job back in L. A. and we haven't been able to talk him out of it. This is just going to give him a nailed-down excuse for hauling us all back to the city. Even if I do tell him who—"

"Which you will not." Burnett eyed her straightly. "This is Wayne's business; he's got to handle it. So trust me a little while, and start developing that quality so rare in womankind, namely, a golden silence."

It was silence, all right, but more the steely type that hung thick over the Ford trailer all that day as Christie and her mother made half-hearted gestures toward packing. Dad hardly spoke. He hadn't told Slater of his intentions; said he was not one to pass out an ultimatum. He would simply wait and see. Meanwhile, he spent the afternoon washing the trailer and car, a sure sign that he was getting ready to travel.

Next morning he was up before six—a positive distress signal! When Christie heard his voice, she scrambled into her clothes pellmell and hurried to join them in the front of the trailer.

Her parents were standing at the window.

"That's strange," Mom marveled.

"Nothing strange about it," Dad stated flatly.

Christie, coming to look over their shoulders, was

158

surprised to see an untidy vacant space next to theirs. The McKinneys had gone, leaving a clutter of junk behind.

"Not strange at all," Dad repeated firmly. "Mac shared my views on this particular subject. He told me some time ago that they would move on the next time a theft occurred. What is surprising is that they stayed this long. Or that we have!" His blood pressure evidently had soared at the sight of Burnett, who at that moment had come out in back of the garage to wash something in a can of gasoline there. The redheaded man was working on Pete's car every spare minute he had these days.

"And I suggest," Dad was going on hotly, "that we lose no more time in following their example."

Christie confronted him as he turned. "Dad, couldn't we just stick around a—a day or two?"

"We could not. Stella, will you please fix breakfast while I take the awning down?"

Woefully Christie followed her mother to the kitchen. For some reason Mom seemed as upset as she was. For a minute she just stood there, glaring at the jar of pickles in her hand as if it had done something outrageous.

And then, from outside, they heard a yelp. Christie thought Dad must have smashed a finger in the folding chair. When they burst out into the patio, they found him standing there, livid and babbling.

"The radio . . . radio . . . MY RADIO'S GONE!"

"Oh, dear! I knew we were going to forget to bring it in one of these nights," Mom groaned.

159

"I'm going to get to the bottom of this if I have to call the State Highway Patrol and have somebody hauled off to jail!" Dad barged off toward the station.

Mom was still dressed in a brunch coat; as she rushed back inside to change, Christie followed her father. Slater never opened up this early, so there could only be one place—one person for whom Dad was heading. As he went around the front of the building, Christie took a short cut through the laundry, stopping short of the passageway as she heard him come into the garage, just beyond. Standing dead-still, she held her breath.

"Morning," she heard Burnett say carelessly.

"If you'll stop attempting to look busy, you and I have something to discuss," Father stated coldly.

"Possibly. But are you in the mood for discussion? You seem fairly steamed up."

"When stealing becomes a commonplace nightly activity in a community of people, everybody should get steamed up!"

"More practical to take steps to stop it," Burnett remarked. "Either call in the law or cast out the spoiler."

"Exactly," snapped Ford. "Which do you prefer?"

"Well"—Burnett apparently was considering the problem unhurriedly—"the law has a fairly heavy hand. I've noticed that justice by court seems sometimes to suck in the innocent bystander almost to the point of penalty. Even being a witness is an embarrassment to some people. Wayne, for instance, has an abhorrence of becoming involved in any legal action."

160

"You've got an agile tongue," Dad yelled, "but you're not talking your way out of this one."

"What am I supposed to be talking my way out of?"

"The innocent act fools nobody! My radio is gone. I want it back. I want it back at once or—"

"All right," said Burnett, "I'll go call Wayne. He's got the keys to the office."

The silence was thunderous. Apparently Burnett actually started out because Christie heard her father say, "Wait a minute! Wait—You mean my radio is in the office?"

"Yes. That seemed like the logical place for it after we recovered it last night."

"Recovered—?"

"I should say we persuaded Mr. McKinney to relinquish it. He was noticeably embarrassed at having been caught in the very act of lifting something. As a fairly accomplished thief, he should have known that Wayne would be watching him after having asked him to leave. But apparently he couldn't resist your radio. And then, too, he didn't count on my having been stationed as lookout."

"McKinney?"

"All along. If you hadn't been so busy pinning labels on me, you might have suspected him yourself." Burnett's tone was losing its mildness. "To raise such a racket over a flashlight? And the pious talk about loving to pay taxes? Practically everything I ever heard him say stank with falseness. Didn't you ever listen to him

161

with any degree of skepticism? Or did you just pin a label on him, too? Does a 'union made' tag guarantee the product?"

"Well"—Dad fumbled—"I never particularly liked the man, but a thief—?"

"Holy heaven!" Burnett exploded. "You should have known he was a crook by his attitude. There isn't a person in this camp he hasn't sneered at for working too hard. He's not only stolen the wages he draws from countless employers, but he has undoubtedly spread his poison to thousands of other workers, who have found it's a fact: He can draw as much pay by not working hard as they can by sweating. If you couldn't pick McKinney out as a cheating, lying, double-dealing grinner, what the devil were you doing, running a business of your own?"

"I think," Ford said in injured tones, "that is a question I do not have to answer to you."

"And I think it is. I think you owe it, after having burst in here, pointing a finger at me." There was a compelling ring in Burnett's demand. "I'm curious about businessmen these days. I've applied for jobs where I've been forced to fill out a whole psychiatric examination. The questionnaires have even asked such ridiculous questions as 'Do you drink?' and 'Are you happily married?' They might just as well have asked 'Are you honest?' Even a lardbrain like McKinney can guess the right answers. Is that how you hired your men, Ford?"

Dad spluttered. "For your information, the irrespon-

162

sible worker is in such predominance today—"

"Baloney! People aren't born lazy. If they loaf, it's your fault for not finding out what makes them want to work. Most people respond to some sort of incentive. You must have been pretty lazy yourself, not to delve into it, study your men. This is a perfect example; here you've spent months buddying around with McKinney when you should have been trying to find out why a bright kid like Joel would rather pick cotton than pick his brains, working for you and your brethren. Don't cry on my shoulder about there being no more good men and women in search of jobs. If you think that, it's no wonder you ended up with a rundown, tin-whistle merry-go-round—stuck with a bunch of wooden horses going no place. Ford, it's a good thing you went broke."

"I did not go broke!"

"All right. Then changed categories. Call it what you please, but I say it's a good thing. Now you'll have to go out and work for somebody else, see how the other half lives. That's undoubtedly what you should have been doing all this time."

Christie turned, aghast, to face her mother, who had come up quietly; together they listened for Dad's answer.

"And I tell you," he came back slowly, "that the economy needs good men who aren't afraid to risk their money and effort in competitive enterprise. Just because I've taken time out for a reappraisal, that doesn't mean I've given up. Mr. Burnett, you just drop around

163

and see me about a year from now. I'll be in business. I'll even show you how it's done."

The two eavesdroppers were retreating; by common consent they ran for the trailer, but there was no guilt in it. They both looked strangely elated.

"He did it on purpose," Christie marveled breathlessly. "Did you see how he did it?"

"What I don't understand is how he knew—I mean—to say that about the job—?" Mom gasped. "Even Mr. Burnett couldn't be that intuitive."

"No. I told him—yesterday. It just slipped out."

They got inside safely—no sight of Dad yet. A moment later he came around the garage, walking slowly.

"What do we do now?" Christie whispered.

"I don't know—I don't know"— Mom started to dither and clamped down on it. "But we've got to help. One little argument won't fix everything permanently. It's one thing to lash back at somebody and another to follow through. If I could just get him to talk to us about it— Oh, heavens, I haven't made the cocoa yet!" She scurried into the kitchen.

Christie stood watching her father; she was thinking about this honest yeast that Burnett had mentioned once. It was going to be hard to do, because it could mean they might leave at once, after all, and that fear was like an ache inside her. But for the moment there was a bigger feeling as she studied the man walking home a little heavily, his face knit hard, the bald spot shining as if

164

from sheer intensity. For the first time in her life Christie knew she had something important to do that might even save them. The knowledge was like a stone floor under her feet.

When Dad came in, he looked at them from deep in the middle of his thoughts. "The radio is safe," he reported tonelessly. "The thief was not Mr. Burnett." It was all the admission he wanted to make just then, and they didn't press him.

Silently they sat down at the table; Dad drank his canned orange juice as if it possibly contained poison. Christie waited until the hot chocolate was poured. Tasted hers. Then, innocently, held her cup at arm's length for an instant, eying it critically.

"Steady," she remarked. "I'm as steady as a frozen fish." Then looking from one to the other of her startled parents she added, "Since I'm not going to have a nervous breakdown, after all, couldn't we have coffee this morning?"

The question lay there like a time bomb, while Mom and Dad shot accusing looks at each other.

"No, neither one of you spilled the cookies," Christie rushed on. "I've known about it ever since we left Los Angeles, and you're pretty wonderful, to haul me out here and keep me from turning into a screaming meemie, but I just thought the time had come to quit having secrets from each other." If it wasn't exactly graceful, at least it chopped through the freeze.

"But how did you learn—?" Dad stammered.

165

"It was an accident." Briefly Christie sketched it for them. "But I do think that doctor didn't give me credit for much gumption, telling you I couldn't stand the truth."

"All this time. . . ." Mom looked as if she might cry.

"I kept still because you kept still," Christie said, "but it seems to me we'd all be better off to level with each other."

"How do you feel?" Dad asked incredulously. "I've thought, lately, that you were looking a good deal better."

"I feel fine. I guess the desert routine worked. I even wish we were staying on here, at least a little while longer."

"Until a certain party comes back," Dad surmised knowingly. "But that might be a long wait, Chris."

It had been years since Dad had called her that—or spoken in any such easy, straightforward way. Christie dug deep into the yeast again.

"I know it, Dad. Of course, I think Joel will come. But that's not the only reason I wish we could stay. It's just that I kind of dread going back to—to the way things were before."

"So do I," her father agreed. "That was one reason I've been considering the idea of getting out of competitive enterprise."

"No!" Christie and her mother said it together.

"That's not what was wrong, Dad! It was everything else, but it wasn't that."

166

"Well, I must say I've always felt that—next year might be better, as they say." He grinned dryly. "But I hate to ask my family to bear with me for another attempt at a game I haven't done well at."

"But we'd love to bear with you!" Mom burst out ardently. "And if you—we—if we ran it differently, Sam—"

"Now, Stella, that's my headache. I don't want you to concern yourself over these matters; it's my responsibility to support the family."

"Sam, do you think I *can't* think?" Mom demanded. "That's exactly what's been wrong all these years, all of us going off in different directions. I had to muddle around, making up programs for the Garden Club, because I didn't ever have anything else to do. The reason I was a good chairman—I *was* a good chairman, Sam— is that I've got ideas. But I could have such better ones if there were any real point. Oh, Sam, I feel so competitive!" It was as if all the dry powder stored up inside Mom was going off in skyrockets.

Dad blinked a little, but you could see the spirit sparking him. "Hold on a minute." He grinned. "If we're going to have a Board of Directors' meeting, let's make that pot of coffee!"

Christie watched them rustling around the stove, elbow to elbow, stealing shy glances at each other that they didn't think she could see. She felt proud and a little weak. And terribly lonely.

16

When Christie awakened that next morning she resisted an impulse to get right up. Instead, she lay in bed, wistfully happy for the new note in the voices that filtered in from the front of the trailer. Mom and Dad were really in orbit. To judge by the snatches of conversation, she was fitting him out with thermoses and sandwiches as if he were going to the forty-ninth state instead of just taking a day's trip.

The small-town idea was Mom's; Christie was a little amazed at the amount of study her mother had given to the subject. She was positively loaded with statistics, approaches; she'd even confessed that she had been reading the financial pages of the paper all these weeks. That was a gruesome prospect, and yet if it worked—at least Dad was listening to her at last. Instead of the twitter on one side and silence on the other, they were having a real discussion in there.

Christie wondered what it would be like to live in a little town. Her mind didn't close with horror as it once had at the very thought. Now she could imagine that under the right circumstances it might even be nice—going to church on a Sunday, with a good man at your side, a couple of kids by the hand, little boys with dark, straight hair well brushed. In a small town you could be important, too—get on the school board, maybe, and ask some questions about why some classes have to be so dull. Or if your husband could turn out to be mayor, you could unpass some of the lousy laws. It could be fun. You'd have a voice in things for once.

The car had backed out and gone now; she could get up. Mom's moment of triumph was over. And yet she lingered, listlessly, until finally she heard her mother tiptoe back. There was a light tap at the door.

"I'm awake," she called.

Mom looked in. She was bright as a poppy this morning. There was some mysterious inner glow in the smile she was smiling.

"Get up, lazy bones," she chuckled. "There's work to be done."

That was nonsense, of course. Out here there never was any work that *had* to be done. "Such as what?"

"I'm busy cooking, so I want you to wash the windows for me." Mom fidgeted into the room, looking as tiddly as a girl with a secret.

"Dad washed them yesterday." Christie yawned.

"He did the outside. The inside's a fright." Mom picked up the shirt and jeans that hung on the closet door and started out with them.

"Hey, wait! What are you—?"

"I'm going to do a big, big washing. So put on a skirt, sweetheart; you hardly ever wear a dress any more. I love you in a dress."

"But Mom! To wash the windows, jeans are better—"

Stella just laughed and went on out of the room, humming a tune.

Feeling tolerant and slightly more aged than a certain parent, Christie got up and dressed in a little blue-flowered wraparound that made her look as feminine as a picture in a Sears, Roebuck catalogue. But if that was what Mom wanted, this was her day.

She went on up to the front of the trailer to find it fragrant with lemon-and-vanilla perfume. Her mother looked up from the cake batter she was mixing.

"There's my little girl, all prettied up. I do hate to ask you to do the windows on a nice morning like this, but you should see how they need it!"

Suspiciously, Christie went to see what was so all-fired awful about the windows, spread the curtains impatiently, and—splintered! All in fragments she stared at the good old beat-up trailer sitting across the way next to the Morenos', a little dustier, a few less shreds of

170

paint— Still speechless she swung around to catch Mom grinning, not the least bit ashamed of herself for having held out.

Rushing across the room with gathering momentum, Christie scooped her mother into a hard hug. "I'll wash the outside of the windows again!"

"Certainly not!" Mom sounded shocked. "Goodness, when it comes to young men, you girls aren't nearly so sophisticated as my generation was."

"But a boy like Joel you have to encourage. He's very shy, Mom. You don't know—"

"Of course I know. He's the old-fashioned kind— they don't like to be flirted with. They want to make all the moves. Exactly the kind I always liked best. I was so afraid when you got stuck with Rudy you'd never have a chance to meet any of the more interesting varieties."

"Well, I never exactly thought I was stuck," Christie said, frowning. "I mean—you know, you like to belong to somebody."

Mom went back to her cake, pouring it expertly into the pan. "There's plenty of time for that—a whole life-time. When I was your age, we all wanted to be pur-sued. The more the merrier. I must say it kept the boys on their toes, not to know they had you sewed up." She ducked the cake into the oven. "Now when the timer goes off, take the pan out and let it cool. Here's the plate to turn it out on. Icing is in that bowl. And don't forget to count ten after Joel knocks."

"Where are you going?" Christie demanded, as her mother picked up a little packet that looked very much like a lunch. She was heading for the door.

"I'm going for a walk," Mom said, as blithely as if she did it every day. "I'm just going to roam out over the desert."

"But what am I supposed to do? I mean—"

Mom was laughing now. "For goodness' sake! You stay here and—cook!"

The cake was out of the oven and iced before Christie caught sight of Joel. He came out of his trailer and went up to the station. Of course that was understandable: going to pay back the loan, pay up the rent for . . . how long?

He seemed to stay a long time. From her post behind the curtains Christie waited like ten thousand bricks ready to fall.

When he finally appeared again around the far corner of the garage, he looked angry. Striding along, thumbs hooked into the pockets of his Levis, face set, he was making straight for his own trailer. And with a strange inner certainty Christie knew that her mother had been mistaken this time. What lay between Joel and her went deeper than coquetry—neither was there anything flirtatious about it. She just had to let him know that she was waiting. Christie stepped out into the patio and stood.

When Joel saw her, he hesitated, finally veered slowly

in her direction, evidently against his will. As he came up, she saw that he was bone-tired. It was evident in the way he walked, in the fine lines of weariness that framed his hard-pressed young mouth. The blue eyes seemed more deepset than ever beneath his dark brows, as if he'd squinted into many a blinding sun these past weeks. When he reached her, he still didn't smile, just stood looking down at her as if to make up for all the days away.

"I'm glad you came back," she said quietly.

"I shouldn't have." He made a little helpless gesture. She noticed that his hands were a mass of scratches.

"Was it a bad time?" She tried to ignore his reluctance, whatever the reason.

"No worse than usual. We worked hard. I've got a little money." He seemed to get the words out with difficulty. "So—? Do I live on it happily ever after? Or do I take Burnett up on his invitation to go shoot myself?" The bleak humor with which he spoke was almost as shocking as the words.

"You *must* have had a bad time!" she said, smiling tremulously. "Come on inside. The folks aren't home. We can talk better there."

"Nothing to talk about," he said wearily, but he let her lead him up the two steps and into the cool depths of the trailer. Glancing around, he said, "Your mother would think poorly of me for coming in when you're alone."

"Who do you think cleared the decks when she saw

173

your trailer back this morning?" Christie told him proudly. "Mom's the absolute best! She's all turned on these days—even going to help Dad go in business again. It's wonderful. You should hear her analyze things. She can tell you how last year everybody was feeling bearish and how once things get bullish we'll do okay. Dad's all fired up. The trouble with men is, they don't realize how much we want to help."

She saw a whole world of fondness and longing flare up in Joel's eyes before he could hide it. He took the hand she'd half held out to him—took it in his calloused fingers as tenderly as if it might break.

"Why should you want to help me?" he said wonderingly. "Nobody else ever did except—" He broke off, made a distracted pass with his knuckles across his eyes. "I'm so tired I'm saying things I shouldn't."

"Sit down," she insisted gently. "You do look worn out."

"Haven't been sleeping well."

"I should think with that kind of work you'd sleep like a rock."

"I usually do, but this time I kept thinking, couldn't seem to stop." He leaned back gratefully against the cushions of the divan. "Burnett is right—working with your back doesn't keep your brain from grinding."

"What was that you just said about him?" She pulled up the hassock and sat down close by. "Has he been picking on you again?"

Joel made a small irritated sound. "I went up to the garage to see him about a little business matter; he got

174

to asking questions. I hate to be quizzed, especially by him. He talks and jabs at you, but what does he himself do about anything?"

Privately Christie had her own opinion about what Burnett could accomplish.

"So he got to needling me about being aimless, not trying to get anywhere." Joel laughed mirthlessly. "He thinks all he has to do is heckle people enough and they'll stiffen up and take on direction, if only to go opposite to him. Maybe it works sometimes, I don't know. But I wasn't going to let him get under my skin. So he finally suggested that if I don't have the gumption to figure out where I fit in the world, I might as well call it quits—save myself the trouble of keeping alive." Joel closed his eyes. "I think I shocked him for once. I agreed."

The words jolted Christie, too. There was some dangerous undertone of seriousness in the mockery, as if beneath his outward control a furious bitterness seethed.

Anxiously she got up, motioned him to put his feet on the hassock. "Why don't you rest awhile? I'm going to fix us something to eat."

"You just make it harder," he murmured drowsily.

"What? What am I making harder?"

"It's not even fair for you to be able to cook, too." He smiled, but the grimness was still there. "I said you'd be everything a man would want. I hope you get a good one, Christie—a guy who'll know the score and be able to make a good life for you."

Hiding her dismay, she came back quickly. "And I

175

hope I'll get one who'll let me share his worries as well as the fun."

He didn't answer.

I need time, she fretted. This isn't playing out right. Delving into the refrigerator, she gratefully got out the food Mom had taken care to provide. With her own limited knowledge of cookery she knew she would have flubbed, especially under these trying circumstances, with Joel slumped back on the divan, looking like "goodby." The thing that unnerved her the most was that he had ticketed Burnett's secret weapon so accurately. As if determined to complicate things, Joel spoke up from the living room. "Christie, have you ever felt the rough side of having somebody love you?"

She stopped fussing with the food and looked across the divider at him warily.

"No, you haven't." He sighed. "You don't know what a tight spot it can put you in."

"There are some tight spots where two people are better than one," she told him, feeling her way. "Loneliness is the worst."

"No, it isn't. Having somebody depend on you is harder. There are so many things wrong—all the little mean angles that you'd like to smooth over or explain away, but you can't, because they're still there gouging you, gouging whoever is with you. You hurt for two people, you run the risks for two people—or more, if you have a family—"

"Risks are half the fun."

176

"Then take the things you're sure of," he persisted doggedly. "One thing you can be doggone sure of is getting old. In eleven years I'll be an old man. Do you think I could let some girl turn into an old woman eleven years from now? That's what I mean about letting somebody love you. It's rough." The raillery of his words seemed to be directed at some secret self, and yet he was challenging her to argue with them.

"You won't be old until you're ninety!" she said indignantly.

"You don't have the inside information. You haven't been to college yet. Ask one of those smart-nosed little personnel grads. They'll be glad to inform you that a man's old the minute he reaches thirty, regardless of how he feels. Oh, some of 'em might allow you to stay young up to thirty-five, but forty is out. The insurance companies have their pension policies to think of. You ever try to explain to somebody about the pension they're not going to have when they get to be sixty-five, because they can't even get a job at forty?" His voice was growing angrier with every word.

"Joel," she said sharply, "you're absolutely right. It's a bad thing. My father found it out when he went looking for a job. But you can't quit on that account!"

"Can't you? What do you do, dive on in? Take the wife and kids with you and hope they don't drown? You know what I mean. It isn't just two, then; it's three or four of you. I say you've dealt yourself in on one whale of a big game when you let somebody fall in love with you, and the way the world looks to me, you're playing against a stacked deck."

"I don't believe it! Maybe you've had bad luck, but other people have made out."

"Have they? I guess they have, but what did it do to them? Did they turn into cheats and boss's pets? Do they maybe hate themselves and everybody else? I've seen more hate in these years—" He stood up and stared around desperately. "That's why I keep sticking to the fields. At least the vegetables are clean—even the bugs on 'em live clean."

Christie snatched at some words from a long way back—Burnett that day in the sun. "So the bugs are doing what comes naturally! But you're not. And if you don't, you could crack up!"

"Maybe, but it's a cinch I won't crack somebody else up with me. That's why I shouldn't be here now. It tears me to pieces, being with you." He stared at her starkly. "It makes me want to be like other people, just go along and take life easy, settle for any kind of little job so long as it doesn't ever develop into a problem that I can't explain. I wish I was the kind who just wanted to sit home evenings and look at television the rest of my life. But it won't work! I'm not like that! I'm one of those hard-heads who're always asking for trouble. Like Wayne, like your dad. If I don't work for myself, I'm no good. I used to get these ideas—I thought maybe I could run a little model shop, make models the machines couldn't touch. I think I could. But I know that the better you get the more you've got to be able to fight off the vultures—the middlemen, the markups, the mass producers. I can fight with my hands, but I don't know whether I'd be able to outsmart all the wise guys. Especially I'm not going to risk somebody else's life on it. That's why I'm leaving here tomorrow, Christie. It'll be easier on both of us."

"Easy!" She followed him to the door. It was all getting away from her. "Joel, who ever wanted things to be all easy? Except McKinney—"

"Go ahead, think like that. Think of me as a slacker, a goof-off. It'll keep you from remembering how we—" He shoved the screen door open and went out, moving tightly, walking away fast.

Bewildered and smarting, Christie turned into the room at last. Her chance—the only one she was going to get—it was all over. Burnett had warned about it; she could still hear his cryptic words:

". . . trying to break the biggest law of all."

17

Stella wore a sunburned, wind-blown look that next day. Ever since her long walk, the wide, dark eyes had been full of visions.

"Flowers all over the place. They're coming out everywhere. Sam, you wouldn't believe it, but all this little green life is putting out buds. A few are even open, the dearest little yellow and peach-colored—"

Dad looked up from the figures he was scribbling on the back of an envelope. "One of the fellows I talked to yesterday said the desert was coming in bloom. I thought he meant the cactus."

"No, these are real garden flowers. Sam, I do hope we can stay another day or two."

180

Christie held still for the answer. She was standing at the front-room window, watching helplessly while Joel, across the way, tried to get his car started.

"Certainly we'll stay here until we lay our plans," Dad was saying. "They've got to be good ones. You'll both be pleased to learn that I got a fine reception in the little burgs I visited. I talked to bankers, merchants, Chambers of Commerce. They're all crying to get little business that will bring in a small pay roll. No trouble about incentives with the workers, either. They like their little towns, if they can only earn a living there. We'd have low tax rates, plenty of space, and we'd save enough on overhead to pay for a salesroom in a good location in L. A."

He was brimming over. Christie felt a sympathy for his high spirits even through the murk of her own disappointment.

Joel had the hood of his car up now and was staring at the engine. At last he turned impatiently and went up toward the garage. As Christie still stood, waiting to see what would happen, she saw the Señora come out of the Moreno trailer to stand looking after Joel with a trace of the same anxiety. On impulse, Christie let herself out and walked across to join the Mexican woman.

The Señora didn't waste words on meaningless greetings; she knew what was in Christie's mind.

"Have you talked with the boy?" she asked, straight to the point.

"He came over a few minutes yesterday," Christie

said quickly, afraid that at any minute Joel might come back and guess what they were discussing. "Señora, what's the matter with him? He wouldn't even stay for lunch. I don't know what's chewing him out inside. I can't even get him to talk plainly to me."

The dark woman hesitated. "It is not right to tell a man's private story, but perhaps . . . I am worried. I thought time would help, he would come back from the fields more calm. Now I think not so. He has not even come to our home once. Can it be he will go again, without a word?"

"He was planning to leave early this morning. For good."

The Señora took the words literally. "No. This is not good for him to do this."

"What is the matter with him?" Christie repeated. "Do you know why he should be so worked up about getting old, having someone else depend on him? He said things yesterday that didn't make sense."

"I must tell a little." The Mexican woman spoke reluctantly. "We know Joel and his papa ever since they first begin to follow the crops. We know how to do, so we show them the way."

"I didn't know he had a—that his father was living."

"Let me tell quickly. The papa is from the old country a long time ago. Been working in New York, to make toys—fine, beautiful work by hand. But they say is no more need for this in toys now; they make only plastics. The papa all at once has no job. He has no heart
182

for this plastics. So he and the boy come to the West where are many companies, but everywhere they say the papa is too old to get a job. A fine man, strong like Joel. He could not understand. They finally come to the fields. The papa can do this better even than the boy. But it hurts him very deep. He feels a shame that the boy must work so young. I think they had money saved once, but when the mama get sick, it goes. I think since the mama die, the papa has no interest but the boy. He think Joel is a little child that needs him. And the boy was good. He played this game, try to cover up so the papa can't see how bad he feels about it all. This is very hard. Joel is like any man—he wants to fight when a thing seems bad, but always he must pretend to the papa nothing is wrong. Then one day Joel has to fight."

"He told me about that," Christie said numbly. "He landed in jail. I guess that made his father feel worse yet."

"The papa understand. He sees it is a fair fight, but he sees how the boy is no child, and how the pretending has gone on too long." Her expressive face saddened. "I think maybe he is glad at last there is no more need put upon him. One day, only a week before we come here, he take the gun and end his life, out alone in the cotton-field."

Christie swallowed dryly. She couldn't grasp all of the implications, but one phrase rang in her mind: "That's what I mean about having somebody love you. It's rough."

"The boy feels very low," said the Señora. "He feels this is somehow his fault. He has failed his father. . . ."

"But what can I—what can anybody do to change him?" Christie faltered.

"Nobody can change a man. This he must do himself. But he needs to be with people awhile yet. He is afraid. He sees everybody like a danger—like a hurt—" She broke off, looking past Christie, her face showing sudden alarm. "Madre!"

Christie turned and gasped. "Fire!"

Smoke was eddying from under the eaves of the station.

"It must be the grill!" She started for her own trailer, yelled in at the door, "Help, everybody! The station's on fire!" and ran up the court.

Pedro was already on his way; the Señora had stopped to make sure the baby was strapped in her cradle. Even the old men were rattling their shanks toward the building, where flames now flickered ugly bright behind the windows.

"How'd she git goin' so fast?" puffed Charlie Sheets.

"Them dry boards'll go like paper," groaned old Gabe.

Joel ran out through the laundry, carrying a bucket of water which he flung as high as he could on the roof of the power plant next to the garage. Burnett was at the washtub, hooking up a hose to the tap.

As the others came up he said, "Somebody go help Wayne with Mabel."

184

Pedro started around front without question.

"Is she hurt?" Christie cried.

"She started the fire. Last I saw, she was still inside, throwing papers on it." Burnett shoved the hose in Sam Ford's hand. "Keep that playing on the power plant. If the generator goes, the whole works is lost." Joel was back now with the bucket, but Burnett intercepted him. "There's a tap out in front. Get on around there and save the pumps." He himself disappeared into the thickening smoke of the building.

"The propane tanks!" Joel tossed the bucket to Christie and grabbing up the wrench that hung on a nearby hook went to work feverishly, trying to disconnect the bottles of gas that stood behind the store. The wall was smoking dangerously now. Christie watched an instant in frozen fright, then, remembering the gas pumps, she ran. She reached the front of the station in time to see Wayne drag Mabel out. The girl was crying, her thin cheeks streaked with smoke and tears.

"I'm sorry—I'm sorry—" she sobbed incoherently. Pedro helped Slater half-carry her away from the blaze. The Señora came to their assistance and then Pete was back, grabbed a water can, and set to work to help Christie, who was pouring water on the pumps as fast as she could fill the bucket. The canopy was mostly steel; except for patches of smolder, it didn't seem to be catching.

The station itself, though, was a furnace, the roof sagging dangerously. In the heart of the blaze things had

185

begun to pop—tin cans exploded, then a sharper series of retorts that crackled like a trapshoot.

"Please—you get back!" Pedro herded her away. "Gun shells going off. Maybe the tanks go—"

At that minute the roof fell and the building buckled inward in a crash of sparks.

"Where's Joel?" Christie gasped sickly. "And Burnett? He ran back in there!"

Pedro was mopping the sweat and soot from his face with the back of his sleeve. "The tanks don't blow up. I think she's over," he panted.

The fire did seem to be burning out as quickly as it had started, little flames flickering along the blackened bones of the ruin. Slater stood staring at it, dazed.

Ford came up breathing hard. "The power plant is safe."

"Have you seen Joel?" Christie repeated.

Her father nodded. "He probably kept the works from blowing sky-high. Got the bottle gas away from the building."

"And Burnett—?"

"He's indestructible!" Ford grinned. "Managed to haul most of the gadgets out of the garage through the rear door. He's still back there counting noses as if they were your children, Wayne, instead of your grease equipment."

Even as he spoke, the two men came around the building together. Silently they joined the group; Joel looked at Christie with a curious satisfaction.

186

"You have a smudge on your nose," he said.

She got the unaccountable feeling that for the first time since she'd known him Joel was living thoroughly in the present moment. As he glanced around at the smoke-stained troupe of people, he had the look of just coming awake.

Only a few minor cracklings still came from the charred rubble now; where the grille had been, a column of odorous smoke rose. Burnett contemplated it approvingly.

"That'll be the potato salad, the lettuce-and-tomato, the magazines, and fishline and all the rest of the junk that's been cluttering up the place for years." He nudged Slater, who still stood speechless like a person in shock. "Nothing like a good fire to help a man simplify his operations."

The odd lot of tables was assembled again in the Fords' patio, and Stella, at her best, was putting together a makeshift meal for the whole court. The fire had burned out; the Highway Patrol had come and made its report and gone; Mabel had been taken to the house, which, with the old salt cedar, stood untouched by the flames.

The Señora was staying with the girl. Wayne hadn't left her side, either, until finally Ford had gone to try to persuade him to come and eat something. Now, at the front of the court, he showed up with Slater at his side.

187

As the two men walked slowly down the length of the drive, Christie murmured, "Poor Wayne."

Joel didn't answer, but Burnett, standing with them in front of the Ford trailer, took issue with her remark.

He shook his head. "Poor Mabel."

"Why do you say that? To do such a thing as burn her own husband's business! I thought she was the thief, once, after I saw her sneaking around one night, but I never dreamed she'd do anything this awful."

"The poor devil of a girl has been trying to live on hatred for months." Burnett spoke with honest compassion. "She's not just going to hell, she's been walking around hip deep in it already. That night you saw her was probably the time she came out following me on one of my nocturnal prowls. Begged me to take her away from here. Anywhere. And the worst of it is, she doesn't even like me."

"So how did you try to cure her, Burnett?" Joel asked abruptly, turning on him.

The redhead glanced at the boy keenly, seemed about to evade the question, then changed his mind. "I must confess I was at a complete loss."

There was no time to say more. As Slater and Ford came up, Christie was surprised to see that Wayne appeared in good command of himself again. He nodded to them, even smiled a little.

"I've got to thank all of you—everybody." To Burnett he said, "Sam tells me you bossed the show. And"— he looked at Joel—"when I think of those gas tanks—

they could have gone off while you were— You shouldn't have taken such a chance."

"Had to." Joel grinned. "He was inside." He jerked a thumb at Burnett. The dumfounded look on the red-headed man's face was almost worth the whole fire.

Wayne was shaking hands with the others. As the talk went on, warm and easy, a far cry from the last time they had sparred across the festive board, Christie watched, wonderingly. It was as if the whole lot of them was reshaping into a different bunch of people from the ones she'd spent the winter with.

"Listen, Wayne," old Charlie Sheets was saying, "I been thinking. Seeing as how the fire happened to happen the way it did, your insurance probably don't cover."

Slater shook his head wryly. "They don't pay off for the homemade variety."

"Well, me and Gabe was talking, and I says—"

"You never did, consarn it," Gabe butted in. "I said it. I says now look here, we got a little money in the old sock, and it probably won't even last us out our days if we just hang onto it and don't make nothing off it, and—"

"That ain't the point." Charlie poked his sidekick. "The point is, if we got to move into a city it's gonna get spent for no good, and besides we're used to living out here."

"Well, me, I always did want to be one of them stock-holders, like you read about," Gabe insisted. "So that's

189

how come we wondered if you mightn't be willing to sell off a slice of your business about now, seeing you might be able to use some extry cash."

"My business?" Wayne seemed about to laugh, then he looked at them wide-eyed. "You don't really mean it?"

"Sure. It don't take much to put up a building out here, just a bunch of boards and what-all." Gabe's old eyes crinkled with anticipation. "By jing, we'd be 'builders,' then, too. A regular 'building and investment corporation.'"

Slater looked around at the others. "Will somebody tell these fellows what a lousy proposition they're trying to buy into?"

Pedro said mildly, "Sound like a good thing—like they say—to get in on the ground floor, no?"

Ford nodded. "It wouldn't take much capital to put you back in business, Wayne. The pumps only got scorched a little. A couple of partners could help you run the place so you could take a day off once in a while. Maybe if you could take Mabel to town for a show every week or so—"

Wayne fiddled with his thumbs. "I don't know. Mabel—" He took a deep breath. "I guess I ought to take her back to the city. But we've got everything sunk in this. She was all for it, too, once. I guess lately I've been working too hard, didn't notice how nervous she's been getting. She wanted to go for a week end in L. A. For a year now she wanted that, but I kept putting her

190

off. Now, I guess it's too late."

"It doesn't have to be," Stella put in timidly, but they listened. "I mean," she went on, picking up courage, "it might help if you brought her over here now. She could sit down with us and take part in the plans."

"Thank you, ma'am." Wayne looked doubtful. "I'm afraid she wouldn't come. She's got it through her head how everybody is down on her. Especially now. . . ."

As he was talking, some sixth sense made Christie think back to that first encounter. Turning to the boy at her side, she touched his arm.

"Joel, you could do it."

He looked down, puzzled.

"You've always stood up for her," Christie insisted softly. "Even when she was being nasty. Don't you re-member? And she stood up for you. You don't know. She told me off when she thought I was just flirting with you. She must feel a liking—maybe because you were both so lonesome. I'll bet she'd trust you if you went and asked her to come here."

"But I hardly know her," he protested in a hushed voice.

The others around the table were listening. They'd heard part of what Christie said.

Wayne nodded. "It's a fact, Joel. She always did have a soft spot for you. You want to go try? It's hard to make her listen—"

Coloring up, the boy shrugged. "If you say so, Wayne."

Christie would have given a lot to know what Joel said the long minutes he was gone inside the adobe house. When he came out, Mabel was with him. So was the Señora.

The way everyone clustered around the red-eyed girl there were reassurances enough being handed out. Christie was certain that her own wouldn't add anything. Mabel would never feel any friendlier toward her; she accepted it without any feeling of bitterness. Working her way around the group, she came to stand beside the Mexican woman.

"How did Joel make out?" she asked quietly.

The Señora smiled. "He talked well. I am glad he could still speak so, of hope and friends."

18

The dead bush beneath Christie's window seemed suddenly to have come alive. In the heart of its dry branches a white flower had bloomed, like a star. It took a minute for Christie to realize that the fragile blossom actually sprang from a slender green stem of its own. The bush was only a shelter. The strange companionship seemed mysterious and beautiful. But then everything this morning was taking on new depth.

Luxuriously she brushed her hair, remembering how Joel had stroked it with his work-roughened hands last evening. So shy, he hardly knew the way to tell a girl that she meant a lot, that he wanted her to be his. He'd talked mainly of his plans, but with Joel that was

193

enough. It was more than enough.

"Christie," he'd said, "those old fellows make me feel like a piker. Risking their little bit in a joint venture at their age. I just wish my father could have known them; he never did understand Americans." And then, just naturally, the story had come out—the story she already knew. But much more of it. He told her everything, all the little parts that had added up to three years of living on a tightrope. "But it's over. I've got to quit playing it back, like I've been doing. I hardly know where to pick up—it's been so long since I left school; if I go back now, I'll be an odd number. But I guess that's the starting place. To finish high. Maybe I ought to go on, at least try out a year or so of college. Do you think it'll help me meet the competition, when I do get out running my own business?"

It meant being apart, of course; they both knew that. To get some night job that would pay the rent while he went to school, Joel said flatly, Los Angeles was the only place to turn. And right away.

"—and I guess you'll be heading in some other direction?" But this time they could face the separation without flinching. Now there'd be good memories to steady them both. Those last few minutes when he'd held her tight, just before he'd said good-by. When she felt the longing about to swallow her up, she set the scene aside to be remembered in another while, when the sting had gone out of it.

Going in to join her parents, Christie found her father

194

talking about Joel. "That's a strange young man. He seemed to open up a little yesterday after the fire. Now this morning—gone. Christie, where did that boy get off to? I wanted to talk to him."

"He had to leave right away for the city," she said. "He's going to try to get in on the second semester. It's not very far along yet. He's decided to finish school."

Mom looked over, telegraphing sympathy, but Christie was able to smile.

"Well, it looks as though everybody's coming into a state of decision," Dad was going on, unaware of the woman exchange. "The question before our house is whether we should try a whole new way of life. Or should we go back to L. A. where we know the ropes? There may be pitfalls in a small town that we aren't aware of. Not much excitement—or—at least— Well, it might turn out to be interesting. A good deal less pressure, more time to try things out. I've even thought I might get back to making some furniture myself again. I once thought I was a pretty good designer."

"I used to love your chair, Sam!" Mom looked ready for anything.

"How do you vote, Chris?"

Startled to find herself invited to join in the policy-making, Christie was a little flustered. For one fleeting thought she yearned for Joel and the nice easy dating they might have had if they had lived close in the city. Then she put it from her. There'd be week ends . . . summertime to come.

"I vote for trying something new." But what she was really saying was, I vote for you two.

Leaving them to their plans, Christie walked out along the court. She could see the haze of color beginning to spread over the desert—tinges of yellow and blue. Butterflies, too, were beginning to prick the gray land with their own flickering brightness, little white ones that blew along the ground like scraps of torn paper, and up above, the big painted ladies swooped in long circles. The sky was rolling slowly—the earth, too, seemed to turn beneath her feet. Christie leaned back against the fresh breeze that ushered her toward the front of the court.

Wayne and the old men were holding a conference over the blackened ruins of the station. To one side Mabel sat, putting polish on her fingernails. The hair was in pin curls again, so Christie was fairly sure there was no need to worry about her—at least for a while.

And then she halted short. A little distance down the highway stood a man with a blanket roll, his russet hair bright as combed copper under the sun. Occasionally, when a car came past, he stuck out a thumb. When he saw Christie running to catch up with him, Burnett unslung the bundle and set it down, waiting for her.

"What are you—? Where are you going?" she demanded, as she reached him. She hardly knew what made her feel so lost at the thought of his leaving.

"Where? You mean literally, physically where?" He

196

looked blank. "My dear, I haven't the faintest idea."

"But why are you running off like this?"

"I don't run off, little one. I run to."

"To what?"

"To whatever comes next. Maybe another fire to help put out. More likely some that need starting."

"But right now?"

"Right now is the time. Don't ask me why. I never know why I feel that a train whistle is suddenly for me."

"You're not going to jump another train!"

"Not here. I'll hitch-hike to the next freight stop and pick one up there. I do prefer to travel by rail."

"But you can't just quit. What will Wayne do without you?"

"He'll do fine. It's invigorating to start to build something." He sounded a little wistful. "I gather Joel was of a similar frame of mind when he left this morning. He wasn't even sore when I replaced the connection that I borrowed from his car the other night."

"You mean you swiped something to keep him from starting off yesterday morning?"

"A little wire to the distributor. Without it, the engine is stopped in its tracks. Easy to connect again if you know how." He studied her affectionately. "I wish I knew how you did it yesterday."

"I didn't do anything."

"Joel's motor was running this morning."

"He just—kind of—woke up. The fire, maybe. He's been in a bad dream. You don't know how bad."

197

"Don't tell me his secrets, even though I'd give a good deal to know them. I could guess their dimensions, though, when he agreed with me that he'd probably be better off dead. That gave me quite a turn yesterday. I was afraid I'd needled him too far. That's the particular danger of my calling; you prick a sensitive person and he'll probably strike back at you, which is as it should be. Makes him rally his strength. But poke someone who's hollow and he'll collapse. As a rule I try to keep from prodding young people before they've had a chance to decide whether they're going to be people or bubbles." He turned back to the road.

Needing to hold him a moment longer, Christie begged, "But why do you have to do this? What is it to you? When you first came here, Wayne said that the only reason you would give was something about gathering stones together."

"Did I? Yes, I guess I did." Burnett looked startled.

"But what does it mean?"

"I've been trying to figure that out the better part of my life. What does a piece of music mean that rocks you? I can't explain it, but you can read the passage if you like. Maybe you'll hear the same music." His pale eyes were vivid with emotion.

"What passage?"

"Ecclesiastes, third chapter." He said it as if she should know what he was talking about. "Or maybe you don't have an Old Testament handy. Your mother didn't seem to recognize the 119th Psalm."

198

"Was that—?"

"The smoky bottle. Tell her where she can find it, if you will. She may need it again someday."

Christie stared at him, stunned by sudden recognition. "You sound like a preacher!"

Burnett almost winced at the word. "No, I did hope to be once, but I was weighed in the balances and found wanting. It takes faith and righteousness to try to walk ahead of one's fellow man, and my own store of those commodities has been seriously depleted. Though I must say that you and Joel have contributed to my dwindled optimism." He made the gesture with his thumb again, and a car coming toward them began to slow.

"No! Wait!" Christie bit her lip. For some reason her vision had suddenly blurred.

"Thank you," he said quietly. "Not many people have shed a tear at my departure."

She brushed at her eyes hastily, but when she could see again, she was standing alone beside the highway. The car was moving off at a good clip. As she stood there, deserted, a swirl of breeze caught up to her—high overhead a handful of butterflies were swept together by it. They seemed to touch before they were driven apart again by the wind.

To everything there is a season,
and a time to every purpose under heaven:
A time to be born, and a time to die;
A time to plant, and a time to pluck up that which is
planted;
A time to kill, and a time to heal;
A time to break down, and a time to build up;
A time to weep, and a time to laugh;
A time to mourn, and a time to dance;
A time to cast away stones, and a time to gather stones
together;
A time to embrace, and a time to refrain from embrac-
ing;
A time to get, and a time to lose;
A time to keep, and a time to cast away;
A time to rend, and a time to sew;
A time to keep silence, and a time to speak;
A time to love, and a time to hate;
A time of war, and a time of peace.

Ecclesiastes 3:1–8